Cynthia Smart's Midwife Crisis

LIZ DAVIES

Chapter 1

Cynthia Smart stared at the word on the little stick of plastic with a growing sense of disbelief.

She could not be pregnant.

It simply wasn't possible.

Rather, it *was* possible, she conceded, but only remotely. Therefore, there must be some mistake. The pee stick must be faulty. It was a false positive. A bad batch.

She'd been horrified enough when, after searching online for the reason for her lack of periods, she'd read that after forty years of age the absence of a period for three months was most likely due to the start of the menopause. Perimenopause, it was called. However, Cynthia was nowhere near ready to accept encroaching middle age.

Of course, the advice was to first consider if there was any possibility she might be pregnant; and she'd assumed there wasn't. She simply couldn't be. But just to be on the safe side, she'd bought a couple of pregnancy tests on the way home from work, to rule it out once and for all. If it was negative, then the advice was to wait a couple more months, because at her age (she didn't appreciate the connotation – forty-four was still youthful), a woman's menstrual cycle can become a bit patchy. If her periods hadn't restarted in that time, she'd need to visit the doctor who would take some blood samples and run a few tests.

Now, though, it looked like her periods weren't set to make a reappearance for at least six more months.

She slumped back against the cistern and hitched in a ragged breath.

Pregnant.

It didn't seem real. How the hell could a one-night stand result in such a life changing event? *I mean, I know how*, she thought, but who could have anticipated it? She was forty-four, her fertile years were well behind her – *and* they'd used protection. Plus, it had only been the once. Twice, actually, but on the same wild, uninhibited night, so it essentially only counted as once.

Up until this point, her memory of the night she had spent with Stan (young, hot, surfer Stan) had been a naughty little secret she'd stashed away in the back of her mind to be brought out now and again when she needed to cheer herself up.

She'd been in California on business and had taken the opportunity to tag a couple of days holiday on at the end. She often did that. It was a great way of seeing a whole variety of places whilst not having to shell out for flights; although she was scrupulous in paying her own accommodation for those non-business days, because there was no way she'd give the Pitbull any opportunity to haul her over the coals.

Stan had been her delicious, golden, twenty-seven-year-old fling. They'd been ships passing in the night, knowing nothing about each other and not wanting to know. It had totally been about the sex and the passion and nothing else. He had no last name and she didn't even know whether Stan was his real forename. All she knew was that he was Australian, and she'd reacted to him like a woman twenty-years younger, all hormones and fluttering nether regions.

She should have stuck with the car.

The BMW was supposed to have been her nod to the midlife crisis she thought she might be going through. The brand-new two-seater BMW in cherry red was a statement car, and the message it sent was that she had made it, financially and professionally. It also said she was a woman to be reckoned with and she was secure in what, and who, she was. There was also the subliminal message that she only needed two seats because there were no children to be taken into account. She also hoped it shouted she was young (ish), single, and carefree.

Well, the carefree bit was clearly about to change, wasn't it?

God, she still couldn't believe it. Her, a mother at forty-four, with no husband (not that she wanted one, thank you very much), a high-powered, demanding job and—

What the hell was the Pitbull going to say when she told him? He would be furious. He wouldn't show it, of course (he wouldn't lay himself open to a potential lawsuit on the grounds of discrimination against a pregnant woman) but she'd be able to tell. After all, her lack of children and her boss's knowledge that she had no desire to add to the world's population, was one of the reasons she'd risen so high in his company. Plus the fact that she was extremely good at her job. *Extremely good.*

Tears pricked her eyes. What an unholy mess. She had no idea what she was supposed to do now, or where she was to go from here. She guessed the first thing she needed to do was to pay a visit to her GP, but she couldn't face the thought of making an appointment and having to explain why she was there. And the subsequent antenatal appointments filled her with horror as she imagined sitting amongst all those other pregnant women, who would undoubtedly be awash with anticipation and excitement, with their bulging bellies full of babies and promises.

Joining their ranks was an anathema to her, and it was definitely not in her five-year plan.

What *had* been in her five-year plan was a promotion. The Pitbull might own the company, but he was getting old. Slowing down. Becoming cautious.

Unlike her. She was still mean and hungry, and she had so desperately wanted to attain the giddy heights of being the chief executive officer of the Webber Corporation.

She still did.

But it wasn't going to happen now, was it?

Although…?

A woman these days had options. Choices.

Should she consider them?

Could she?

As she sat there on the brilliant white loo seat in her brilliant white-tiled bathroom, with its gleaming chrome and stainless steel, and towels large enough to lose oneself in for a week, she imagined how it would look with a child in it. A little girl playing happily in the bath, surrounded by froth and bubbles. A little girl with glossy thick hair, the colour of a raven's wing, the same colour as her own (she ignored the grey strands at the temples which she was forced to dye). A child with grey eyes and freckles across her nose. A child who was the spitting image of herself when she had been that age. Looking like a young Cynthia and displaying no hint of the man who had fathered her.

Her child. Her daughter. Hers.

And she knew she didn't have a choice, because the decision had already been made. Her heart had spoken, and she had heard it loud and clear.

She was going to have this baby, and it had better look exactly like the little girl in the bath.

Chapter 2

The Pitbull, aka Ricky Webber, glared at her. Cynthia could feel his eyes boring into her, and she shuffled in her seat, keeping her attention on her laptop and swallowing nervously. She was certain he knew her secret and he weighed her down with his unspoken disapproval and disappointment.

She was aware she was being silly. There was no way the Pitbull could know. No way. She'd not even made an appointment with her GP yet, although she had peed on another three or so sticks, just to make sure.

They'd all told the same story.

At least her figure wasn't giving the game away yet. She was as svelte as she had always been, her boobs still hardly more than lemons planted on her ribcage. And she hadn't been sick either, nor had she felt in the slightest bit nauseous. There had been no excessive tiredness, no cravings (maybe that came later?), no increased hunger. Apart from the absence of her periods and the confirmation on the tell-tale pregnancy test sticks, there was absolutely no indication she was growing another person inside her.

The thought made her grimace, and she wrinkled her nose. It was all a little bit gross and rather reminiscent of something from the Alien movies. She might be looking forward to having a daughter, but the process of obtaining one didn't appeal in the slightest – apart from the very beginning bit where Stan had played a starring role.

Still, for the moment she could pretend it wasn't happening because no one knew her little secret, and she intended to keep it that way for as long as possible – at least, until she'd worked out a game plan which consisted of how to break the news to Ricky and in the same breath convince him she'd covered all the bases.

'Cynthia, wakey, wakey; I'm not running a meditation session,' Ricky barked. 'I need your full focus. *And* your full co-operation.'

'You have them,' she replied, calmly, after taking a deep breath. 'You always do.'

'Good, because I'm expecting excellent results from the both of you.' He snapped his fingers, and she gritted her teeth.

Wait, what? Both of *whom*? She glanced quickly at the rest of the people around the conference table, covering her confusion with a confident smile, trying to send the message that everything was perfectly fine and under control – when, in fact, she didn't have the slightest clue what Ricky was on about.

The other board members met her eye without flinching, but there was no acknowledgement, so she could only assume none of them were the other half of the "both" that Ricky was referring to.

'I've invited him to join us,' the Pitbull continued. 'Max will be here any minute, but I wanted to give you the heads up first. Now, Cynthia, I know how territorial you can be, but I expect you to play nice. He's here to do a job and if you start getting all defensive then the job won't get done. And I don't have to tell you I won't be a happy bunny.'

Bunny? There was nothing cute or fluffy about Ricky. The only thing he and a rabbit had in common was his sexual appetite. And his overly large ears.

Invite who? And "invite" was a polite word for him, because Ricky didn't invite; he ordered, commanded, demanded. *Expected.*

When the door opened, Cynthia was at a disadvantage because her back was to it and she refused to ignominiously wriggle around in her seat. Instead, she waited for Ricky to half rise from his and gesture to the empty chair two seats down from his. It belonged to Jeffrey, who hadn't filled that space for several weeks now, due to a heart condition. Rumour had it he wouldn't be sitting in it ever again if Ricky had his way. The Pitbull didn't accept illness in himself or his employees.

The rest of the board members swivelled their heads or craned their necks.

Cynthia stared serenely ahead and waited for this unknown man to sit down.

Only then did she look at him.

He was a bit of a dish.

'As I said, this is Max Oakland and I've brought him on board to advise on the Field Mouse Project. He knows the hotel business inside out, so he's best placed to collect and disseminate vital information.' Ricky smiled his shark smile, all teeth and no warmth, complete with dead eyes as he scanned the room. His attention came to rest on Cynthia. 'I expect you two to work together. Let's not have any pissing contests.'

'That's hardly going to happen,' she replied, her voice level, her tone cool. 'Nice to meet you, Max.' She inclined her head and gave him a brief professional smile. She wasn't going to let his good looks get in the way of a working relationship. He was incredibly attractive and undoubtedly knew it. She also guessed he would try to use it to his advantage.

'You, too, Cynthia.' His smile was wider and appeared to be more genuine, but she wasn't fooled.

She knew his type. Max Oakland was as much of a shark as Ricky was. Just a bit younger and with fewer teeth. On first impression, he also appeared better at concealing his true nature than her boss was. Mind you, Ricky was rich enough and had enough clout not to have to bother to conceal anything. So maybe Max would be just as forthright and obnoxious when he'd aged a couple more years and had several million pounds in his bank account.

'You two can bugger off and get started,' Ricky announced, as soon as Max had settled in his seat, and Cynthia smiled at the momentary and fleeting disconcerted expression on the man's face. Trust Ricky to assert his authority as soon as the newest member of the team had entered the room. She wasn't happy with the way she was being dismissed, either. Not when she was supposed to be the Operations Director and his right-hand person. He was clearly putting both of them in their place and stamping his authority. The nasty old git.

She waited for Max to get to his feet then she rose to hers, turned smartly on her heel, and swept out of the room. It was the only advantage of sitting with the door directly behind her – she could be out of her chair and down the corridor before most of the others had negotiated their way around the massive table.

'Wait,' she heard Max call, and she reluctantly paused for him to catch up.

Expecting him to want to discuss the project, she was taken aback when he said, 'You don't like me much, do you?'

'I don't know you,' she responded neutrally.

'You think you do. We're similar people.'

Cynthia raised a well-groomed eyebrow (years ago, she'd spent hours perfecting the move in front of the mirror). 'Similar people?' she repeated. 'I don't think so.'

'Believe what you like, but I know for a fact that you're driven, smart – see what I did there?' He chuckled, and she narrowed her eyes at him. 'Competitive and incredibly ambitious.'

'You left something out.'

'Oh?'

'Independent. I don't like working with others.'

He smiled. He was quite charming when he smiled, but she wasn't going to let his good looks distract her.

'Yeah, like Ricky said – you're territorial. But I'm sure we'll muddle along together.'

Cynthia took a deep breath and let it out slowly. 'I do not muddle,' she replied, her voice icy. 'I don't expect you to muddle, either. Now, if you don't mind, I'll get my PA to schedule a meeting with you, say, later today? And I expect you to have your plan for the takeover on my desk a half an hour before then, so I can read it through before the meeting.'

'That is so not going to happen,' he replied.

'*Excuse me?*

'I'm not your lackey. We're in this together, as equals. I'll bring my thoughts to the table, but you must contribute, too. I'd like to hear your take on how we're going to proceed.'

Cynthia could feel her irritation building to outright ire. 'Fine,' she retorted, and whirled on her three-inch high heels and stalked towards her office, feeling his eyes boring into her.

'Sally, set up a meeting with Max Oakland for later today,' she instructed her PA as she marched past her and stormed into her office, anger coursing through her. 'You'll probably find him in Jeff's office.'

She knew exactly what his game was. Ricky had been threatening for months to replace Jeffrey and that was before the poor man had even had the heart attack. She was convinced Max had been brought in with the idea of him filling Jeffrey's shoes, but she guessed Ricky was putting him through his paces first. None of the other directors on the board were a threat to her and her ambition to step into Ricky's shoes when the time came. But her instinct told her Max Oakland was a different proposition. And for the first time in an exceedingly long time indeed, Cynthia felt threatened and more than a little worried.

Chapter 3

Cynthia should be working on her proposal for the hotel chain takeover, but she couldn't concentrate. She was acutely aware she should be throwing everything she had into this – after all, her career depended on it – but every time she tried to focus on the project, the result on that little stick kept coming to the surface. The knowledge that she was pregnant circled relentlessly through her mind, and she found herself tripping over it constantly.

As soon as she'd returned to her office from the meeting, she'd opened a spreadsheet to begin work on the project, but instead had thought about creating a new one to list those things she needed to do to ensure everything was put in place for when she took her maternity leave. All two weeks of it. That should be enough, shouldn't it? When she looked at her online diary, she decided she needed to check when the baby was due. Counting forwards six months she made a mental note of the date; she certainly wasn't going to put anything pregnancy related into her diary for now. Sally was discrete, but Cynthia didn't want anyone, including her PA (a small part of her continued to think it was a mistake) to know yet. Not until she'd had things confirmed by her doctor and certainly not until she was much further along in the process. The less anyone knew right now, the better. She'd seen how Ricky had treated his pregnant staff and it wasn't pleasant.

Not that he did or said anything he could be sued over – he was too canny for that – but pregnant women and those female staff with young children didn't progress in the business. They were gradually managed out, and she had no intention of letting the same thing happen to her.

When would she start to show, she mused, running a hand over her stomach which was still relatively flat. The waistband of her skirt was a little snug, but she could live with that for a while.

Actually, scrap that – it might be an idea to buy a couple of new suits in a size larger now, rather than wait until the ones she currently owned were straining at the seams. Everyone knew tight fitting clothes can make people look fatter than they truly are, and she didn't want anyone to think she'd put on weight. Not that they'd say so to her face, but gossip was rife in this place and she didn't want to start the rumour mill turning.

First though, she needed to make an appointment with her doctor.

Cynthia looked the number up online and picked up her phone. While she went through the various options (there didn't appear to be a "shit-I'm-pregnant" option) she tapped her perfectly manicured fingernails on her desk and worried at her lip with her teeth. Ricky might have brought Max Oakland in as a potential candidate to fill Jeff's seat on the board, but she'd bet her last penny that Max had an agenda of his—

'Oh, hello, yes, I'd like to make an appointment to see the doctor, please,' she said. Disconcerted when the voice on the other end asked her the reason, she huffed, 'Is that any of your business?'

'Doctor likes to have an idea as to the nature of the appointment,' the receptionist informed her.

'It's personal.'

'I appreciate that – all patients' appointments are personal…'

'I'm pre—'

Cynthia slammed the phone down as her PA knocked and walked straight into her office, holding a steaming mug in her hand.

'I thought you might like a cup of coffee…' Sally trailed off when she saw the expression on Cynthia's face. 'Oh, sorry, I…'

'It's OK. It wasn't important.' It served her right to make a personal phone call in her office. She had the type of relationship with Sally which meant Sally was privy to almost everything, and unless Cynthia was holding a meeting in the office, then Sally was free to come and go. 'Thanks for the coffee, it's just what I need.'

Sally placed the mug carefully down on the desk. 'I've set up a meeting for you and Max Oakland at three-thirty this afternoon. Is that OK?'

Cynthia wrinkled her nose. 'Great, thanks.'

'He's a bit of a dish, isn't he?' Sally said, as she gathered up a document from Cynthia's out tray and checked it had been signed.

'You think?' She'd been thinking the exact same thing, but there was no way she was going to admit it to anyone.

'Mmm, he's rather yummy. I like them tall, dark and handsome.'

'He's a bit too up himself for my liking,' Cynthia said. Not to mention he was chasing the CEO job.

'Ooh, I think he's lovely. He answered the phone himself, too.'

'You called him? What's wrong with email?'

'He doesn't have one set up yet, so I called him instead. I've heard a rumour Ricky's given you a new project,' Sally continued, lingering by the door.

'Nothing gets past you, does it?'

'What can I say? The PAs talk… Except for me, of course. I just listen.'

'It's called the Field Mouse Project and you'll be hearing a lot about it in the coming weeks and months. Ricky is planning a takeover bid of a large hotel chain, but it has to be hush-hush because if anyone gets wind of it the share prices will rocket. At least it's in the UK this time, so I don't have to spend half my life on a plane,' she added.

Sally tilted her head to one side and gave her a curious look. 'Since when did you become a home-bod? This doesn't sound like the Cynthia I know and love.'

'I fancy being in the office a bit more, that's all,' she replied.

'Is it because you think the Pitbull is lining Max up to take his place?'

Cynthia cocked her head. Her PA was particularly astute today. 'I hope not, but you can never be too careful, can you?' She picked up her coffee, took a sip and nearly spat it out. 'Ugh.'

'What's wrong with it?' Sally asked, hurrying back to the desk and peering anxiously at the cup.

'It tastes horrid. It smells funny, too.' Cynthia sniffed and wrinkled her nose.

Sally took the cup from her, sniffed, then took a tentative sip from the opposite side of the rim. 'It seems all right to me. Let me make you another.'

'It's OK, I'll just have water. I'll pop to the loo and fill my bottle up on the way back.' Cynthia shook her empty designer water bottle and gathered up her phone. 'I won't be a sec.' Now why did she say that? She only ever told Sally where she was going if she was leaving the building or attending a meeting. She didn't usually make a habit of broadcasting her loo breaks, or declaring how long she was likely to take.

She left Sally staring after her and hurried off to the ladies' toilets where she made another quick call to the doctor's surgery and finally managed to make an appointment for later that day. It wasn't ideal, but now she knew she was pregnant, there didn't seem much point in putting it off. And she knew from past experience there never would be a good time. It did mean though, that she'd have to cut her meeting with Max short, but the silver lining was that at least it couldn't drag out for hours. She'd give him an hour and a half, then she'd have to call time.

As it happened, she found she didn't need that long.

She'd prepared some notes, had done some research, and had a tentative idea of how to proceed, but Max sodding Oakland had only gone and done a presentation, complete with graphs, graphics, and music.

'You do realise I'm the only one likely to see this?' she pointed out. 'It's impressive and it must have taken you all day, but the plan will change at least twenty times before it's approved, and then it still has to be flexible.' But she had to admit his work was sound and thorough, and she was having difficulty picking holes in it no matter how much she tried. It didn't help that her tummy was rumbling and she was so hungry she felt sick, despite the substantial lunch she'd eaten. Her normally razor-sharp brain was a little fuzzy around the edges too, and she was finding it hard to concentrate.

'It took about an hour, that's all, and the plan *is* designed to be flexible,' he informed her neutrally and she wanted to wipe the calm expression off his face.

It was seriously annoying that she couldn't find much at all wrong with it. Of course, it all depended on whether the Webber Corporation would be able to buy the chain outright, or whether they'd decide to cherry pick the best hotels and forgo the others, and it would also depend on whether Ricky's plans would be approved by the various councils and their planning departments. She hadn't seen the details and didn't need to. Her remit was to acquire the company and there was so much to do, and so many things to think about it was making her head spin.

'Are you OK?' Max asked, concern etched on his face.

'I'm fine,' she snapped, wishing her head didn't feel full of cotton wool and wishing she didn't feel quite so nauseous. She'd better not be coming down with something. 'If that's all?' she asked.

'I've nothing more to add at this point, but you might need to consider…'

All Cynthia was hearing was blah, blah, blah as she struggled to keep her lunch down. She'd eaten it early and had wolfed it down, but despite her meal she was feeling both hungry and sick at the same time. Having a potential rival for the position she'd been after for years do such an excellent job in such a short space of time, didn't help either. Worry and annoyance were vying for supremacy in her head right now, and she didn't like it. She wasn't used to feeling anxious and it didn't suit her.

After another hour spent at her desk, still trying unsuccessfully to pick holes in Max's proposal, she finally gave up. It was nearly time for her appointment with her GP anyhow, and she was feeling a little stressed about that. She hardly ever went to the doctor and she was rarely ill, so she wasn't looking forward to her visit. She hated having to relinquish control to anyone else, and she had a feeling she'd be on the back foot; pregnancy was totally out of her comfort zone and she didn't know the first thing about it, or what to expect. So that was another thing she had to add to her to-do list – read anything and everything about being pregnant. She never went into a situation blind, be it purchasing her apartment or dealing with an issue in work, and she had no intention of this being any different. Knowledge is power, so they say.

'Who are you meeting?' Ricky's voice made Cynthia jump.

'No one,' she said.

'You're taking a half day then, are you?'

'Very funny.'

'It's not like you to skive off.'

'It's five-fifteen. I've been at my desk since six-thirty.' She hated sounding so defensive. She'd worked nearly eleven hours straight.

How could she be accused of skiving? She rarely had a holiday, and she was always in earlier than him and waited until he went home before she left. It was almost a game between them – except she was deadly serious and he liked pushing her buttons.

Ricky studied her. 'Are you sure you're not meeting with someone?'

'No, I'm not.' She knew what he meant, and there was no way she was going to change jobs now, not when she was so close to running the business. 'It's a personal thing.'

His eyes widened and his lips twisted into a mocking smile. 'Have you got a date?'

'No.'

'You have, haven't you? Do I know him?'

'I haven't got a date.'

'Then why are you leaving so early? You usually try to outlast me.'

'Because I'm going to visit my mother.' She disliked lying, but he wasn't giving her much choice.

His look was sharp and penetrating. Evidently he didn't believe her. 'Give her my regards.'

Ricky had never met her mother. Ricky probably wasn't even aware she *had* a mother (apart from the very obvious fact that biologically Cynthia wouldn't exist without one) because she never spoke about her personal life in work. Not even with Sally, and neither was she the kind of manager who had to have her PA remember birthdays and anniversaries for her. Cynthia was perfectly capable of remembering those kinds of things herself.

'Will do,' Cynthia said as she breezed past him.

But she was still smarting from his comments when she was called into the doctor's consulting room some half an hour later.

'Ms Smart, what can I do for you, my lovely?'

Cynthia gritted her teeth. 'I thought you'd already be aware.' And please don't call me "my lovely" she wanted to say. The woman was younger than her, possibly in her early thirties, and far too young to be calling her "my lovely", as if Cynthia was some kind of an old dear.

'Why should I be?' Dr Cullen peered at her over the top of her glasses.

'I had to tell the receptionist the reason why I wanted an appointment.'

'Ah, I see. OK, if you could just tell me in your own words why you're here today.'

Whose words would she use, if not her own? God, this was excruciating. 'I'm pregnant.'

'Have you had it confirmed?'

'That's why I'm here.'

'I mean, did you take a pregnancy test?'

'Of course I did. Several, in fact.'

'I'm asking because at your age you can have something known as the perimenopause and that means—'

'I know what it is, and I don't have it.'

'OK, right then, pop your shoes and skirt off, and hop onto the bed so I can have a quick feel of your tummy.' The doctor walked across to the basin and washed her hands.

More gritted teeth, but Cynthia did as she was asked, lying rigid with her hands at her sides and her fingers curled into fists, relief at not having her skirt cutting into her waist tempered by the patronising attitude of a woman so much younger than her.

'I'm just going to ease your tights down a bit. Is that OK?' the doctor asked.

'Go ahead.'

The woman's hands were warm and gentle as she worked her way across Cynthia's stomach, pressing down lightly with a sort of cupping motion.

'When was your last period?' the doctor asked.

'Three months ago.' Cynthia thought for a second. It was before she flew to California (obviously) but how long before? She finally managed to pin it down. 'January 31st.'

'And how have you been feeling? Any pains in your tummy? Any morning sickness? Any weight gain? Bloating? Piles?'

Cynthia shuddered. *Piles?* Dear God. 'I've been fine. The only reason I bought a test was because I'd missed three periods in a row. The first two I put down to stress – my job is incredibly stressful – and I've missed the occasional one in the past. But never three. I didn't expect it to be positive,' she admitted.

'You can sit up now.' The doctor washed her hands again, while Cynthia adjusted her clothing and put her shoes back on.

'Well?' she asked.

'You are definitely pregnant, so the next thing is to book you in with the midwife and arrange to have a dating scan done.'

'A what?'

'A dating scan. It's usually performed anywhere between the eight and the fourteen-week stage, so by my estimate you're slap bang in the middle of that. It will give us a more accurate date of when we can expect your baby to be born.'

Good, because she needed to know exactly when it was due so she could start to firm up her rough plan. As soon as she had a confirmed date, she'd book two weeks off work, then she could calculate backwards from there as to when she'd have to start looking for a nanny.

Right then, time to hit the shops to purchase some new suits. She just hoped the places she usually bought her clothes from were open until eight p.m. because she honestly didn't think she could wear any of the ones she currently owned tomorrow. Leaving the button of her suddenly expanded waistband undone, she headed towards her favourite shop, her mind working furiously.

If she played her cards right, Ricky might not even notice his most capable director was pregnant until after she'd had the baby. And maybe not even then.

Chapter 4

What a day! Just over twenty-four hours ago she had been walking through the door of her apartment, blissfully unaware she was growing another human inside her and busily plotting world domination. Or, taking Ricky's job, at the very least; although, to her, it amounted to the same thing.

Now look at her – pregnant, with a humungous and challenging buy-out to pull off, and being forced to work alongside a man who was clearly meant to be Ricky's replacement.

Cynthia positively seethed with anger at the thought. She'd earned that position. She'd worked herself to the bone for that company; she'd forgone marriage and kids (hold the kid thought for the moment), she'd not gone on holidays apart from the occasional days she tagged onto business trips, she'd abandoned any social life years ago, and she hardly saw her mother – and for what? For the rug to be pulled out from under her feet at the last hurdle, that's what.

She wasn't stupid; she could feel it in her gut and her instincts were rarely wrong. Ricky didn't want her to be the next CEO. The reason was twofold. For one thing, she was female; she might be brilliant at her job but she was a woman, and she'd always known Ricky was a misogynist and a bully. The second was, she knew she'd do as good a job as he did – better probably. He knew it too, and he resented her for it. Oh, and there was a third – Ricky wasn't prepared to retire yet, and probably wouldn't be for another ten years.

Now, though, Max Oakland was on the scene and her radar was on full alert.

Nothing had been said. No one had hinted at anything. The other directors had all seemed as surprised as she had been when Max had waltzed into the board room this morning. But she knew. She'd been watching Ricky's face, and she knew. He was lining Max up for the top job.

She also accepted that once Ricky found out she was in the family way, her days at the Webber Corporation were numbered. Oh, she'd still be working for the company (he couldn't get rid of her, he wouldn't dare), but she'd be gradually side-lined and overlooked until she might as well be opening the post and doing the filing.

Knowing she was justified in keeping Ricky in the dark about her impending motherhood didn't make it any easier to do. She'd have to be very careful – there were only so many times she could say she was leaving early to visit her mother. Of course, despite her wishful thinking earlier, he'd find out sooner or later; but she intended to have all her ducks in a row before that happened.

She'd show him she could juggle both roles; although she hated the term "juggling", because honestly how hard could it be to be both a mother and a successful career woman? People did it all the time. There was absolutely no need to give up work. Not even a demanding job like hers. A suitable nanny would do the trick, and it might cost her a bit in the first couple of years, but as soon as her daughter was old enough for school (when was that – aged three, four?) then the cost should come down significantly.

Removing her purchases from the bags, she hung the suits in the bathroom and gave them a shake. The steam should remove most of the creases. She picked out a pair of shoes, fresh underwear, and a silky blouse in a deep scarlet ready for the morning, and then had a long, hot soak in the bath.

Crikey, she was tired. If she wasn't careful, she might fall asleep in the tub, so she heaved herself out and was just about to dry off when a wave of nausea swept over her. She only had time to take one step towards the loo before she threw up over the bathroom floor. Feeling rather unsteady, she leant against the tiled wall and took a couple of deep breaths. God, she could do with a shower now because she felt all hot and clammy, and there was an extremely nasty taste in her mouth.

She hated being sick. She hated being ill. And she certainly hated the weakness that came with it. Not only that, she didn't have time to be ill.

Wearily, she cleaned up the mess, then had a quick shower before slipping into a pair of satin pyjamas. To her surprise, she was suddenly ravenously hungry again, so she headed for her gleaming, pristine kitchen and delved into the fridge.

There wasn't a great deal in it, apart from some fruit, a block of cheese, some olives, and half a bottle of wine.

On any other evening, she'd cut up the fruit, slice the cheese, and serve it with the olives and some balsamic vinegar, washed down with a glass of chilled white wine. But all she wanted now was pasta. Or potatoes. Bread would do. Anything with carbs in it, basically.

Cynthia never ate carbs. How else was she able to remain slim? But now she craved them so desperately she was salivating. Her eyes widened – chips. Hot fluffy chips, with lots of salt and vinegar, and maybe a piece of battered cod to go with it.

She shook her head to clear the image away and thought about sushi instead. Far healthier and with significantly fewer calories.

But no matter how hard she tried, the thought of raw fish didn't make her mouth water, and now she'd thought about fish and chips, she couldn't stop.

There was only one thing for it – she'd have to have some.

With eager fingers, she looked up the nearest chip shop which had a delivery service and ordered a portion of cod and chips and a carton of mushy peas. Then she poured the wine down the sink, and promptly burst into tears.

There was a horrid feeling hovering on the fringes of her mind that this time she'd bitten off more than she could chew, and the craving for greasy calorie laden food was only the start of her life spiralling out of control.

What on earth made her think she could do this? She couldn't even eat healthily, and this was only the end of day one of knowing she was pregnant. She'd been sick, she was so knackered she could cry, most of her clothes didn't fit, and she'd left work earlier than she'd ever left the place before. Ricky was baring his teeth at her, the new guy had everything going for him (good-looking, intelligent, corporate, male and definitely not pregnant) and she had no one with whom to share her burden. No one who'd massage her feet after a long day in heels; no one to commiserate with her, to sympathise, to make her a cup of peppermint tea; no one to hold her and tell her everything was going to be all right.

She ate her meal, stuffing the chips into her mouth as fast as she could, with tears trickling down her cheeks and a terrible loneliness in her heart.

Chapter 5

Max Oakland was the most irritating man on the planet, Cynthia concluded. If he second guessed her one more time, she was going to scream. Every time she suggested something or pointed something out, he'd already done it, dealt with it, and had got a bloody T-shirt printed.

She had no idea why Ricky had given the Field Mouse Project to her, when it would clearly be better for Max to oversee it all on his own. He was two steps ahead of her and had been all week. And the annoying thing was, he didn't gloat about it. He wasn't smug, and neither did he flaunt it, or rub her nose in it. He was unfailingly nice, and kept asking her opinion and soliciting her input, even though it patently wasn't needed.

The fact that she agreed with everything and had no additional input to… well… *input*, grated on her nerves until she was feeling frayed around the edges and wound up like a coil. Her blood pressure must be through the roof, and she was

28

vaguely concerned all this stress and ire would have an adverse effect on the baby. She couldn't risk any complications, especially not when the Pitbull had announced Jeffery's resignation and had appointed Max in his place.

That was a surprise – *not*.

'That's me done for this morning,' Max said, closing his laptop down and leaning back in his chair. He stretched his long legs out and she flinched as the toe of one of his shoes brushed her ankle.

'Sorry, I didn't mean to kick you,' he said. 'Are you OK?'

'I'm fine.'

'That's a relief. Lara often tells me I don't know my own strength.'

Not that she cared very much or genuinely wanted to know, but she found herself asking, 'Is Lara your wife?'

'Good Lord, no. She's my best mate's wife. I'm not married. Not anymore, anyway. I was once, but it didn't work out, and I've been divorced for nearly ten years now.'

'Any children?' She didn't think she'd ever asked anyone that particular question before – she was more likely to ask where they got their business cards printed, or what car they drove; however, this past week she'd become ever so slightly interested in other people's kids.

'No. You?' he asked.

Oh hell…

She bypassed the question regarding children and went straight in with, 'No, I've never been married. I've not got a significant other, either.'

Why had she felt it necessary to tell him that last bit? It wasn't as though she was broadcasting her single status and hoping he'd pick up her signal. For one thing, she never played around on her own doorstep, and for another she was pregnant, so she most definitely wasn't in the market for a man. Even if the man in question was seriously attractive and was gazing at her as though she was the most important person in the world.

She knew what he was doing as she'd used the same tactics herself, giving her undivided attention to someone to make them feel special and important.

'Fancy grabbing a bite to eat?' he asked. 'I know a great little bistro a couple of streets away.'

'You've been working here all of five minutes and you think you know everything,' she retorted, only half joking. 'If you're referring to Luigi's, I already know it.'

'Then you know how good the food is,' he said, and when she hesitated, he followed it up with, 'It'll only be a quick bite to eat. I'm going for a run after work tonight, so I'll need something more substantial than a sandwich to keep me going.'

Cynthia thought for a moment, before agreeing. Since she'd discovered she was pregnant, she found if she didn't eat regularly she had a tendency to feel sick, and there was also the old adage about keeping your friends close and your enemies closer. It wouldn't do any harm to get to know him a bit better.

'OK,' she agreed, her mouth already watering at the thought of what might be on the specials board.

'I'll grab my jacket and meet you in the foyer,' he told her, and she heard him joking with Sally on the way out.

'Do you want me to fetch you something from the deli?' her PA asked a second or two later, as she popped her head around the door. 'Oh, are you going out?'

Cynthia had her bag slung over her shoulder and her jacket on, although lately she did tend to wear it whenever she wasn't sitting down in order to deflect attention away from her midriff.

'I didn't think you had any meetings for the rest of the day,' Sally added.

'I don't. I'm going out for a bite to eat.'

'You are?'

'Yes, Max asked me to have lunch with him at Luigi's.'

'*Really*? Lucky you.' Sally's eyes were almost popping out of her head.

'It's nothing to do with luck. This is strategy. The better I get to know the man, the easier it will be to take him down. Right, I've got to go. He's waiting for me in the foyer.' And with that, Cynthia darted around her PA and out of the office.

Max was already there. 'Ladies first,' he said, holding the door open for her, and falling into step beside her once she was through.

She set off at a brisk walk, the thought of an avocado and pancetta salad making her stomach growl. Max kept pace beside her, and she was conscious of how tall he was and the breadth of his shoulders. He almost filled the pavement all by himself, and whenever they met someone coming in the opposite direction, he had to step behind her so they could pass.

She kept sneaking glances at his profile, too. He had a nice shaped nose and a strong jaw. When he caught her looking, she said, 'I'm not walking too fast for you, am I?' and she received an amused chuckle in return.

'Is this it?' he asked, when she half-stopped outside a restaurant with pretty window boxes on the sills. She turned and almost bumped into him as he carried on walking before he came to a halt and glanced up at the sign,

'I don't believe it,' she said, when realisation struck. 'You haven't a clue about this place, have you?'

He held his hands up. 'Guilty as charged.'

She shook her head as she yanked the door open and marched inside. He'd played her like a trout on a line, and she couldn't believe she'd fallen for it. Without waiting to see whether he was following, she made her way through the crowded bistro and out into a flower-filled, sheltered courtyard. For mid-May it was wonderfully warm, and after being cooped up in the office all morning, she needed some fresh air.

Choosing a table under a sun umbrella – the sun was surprisingly strong for the time of year – she placed her bag at her feet and began removing her suit jacket before thinking twice. It might be her imagination because she'd only known she was pregnant for just over a week, but she was sure she was starting to show. There was a gentle rounded tump between her belly button and her pubic bone that most definitely hadn't been there eight days ago, and her boobs were bigger, too. They were alarmingly large, in fact. They'd doubled in size overnight, and she wasn't sure how she felt about them. She was so used to having little boobs, that this sudden growth spurt had taken her unawares and she realised she was spilling out of her bra. She hadn't noticed earlier when she was in her office, but whether it was the sunlight or something else, she now saw she had a four-boob thing going on and it wasn't the least bit attractive.

Hoping Max hadn't noticed, she shrugged her jacket back on and picked up a menu, even though she knew exactly what she was going to have. Along with the salad, she might have some rye bread, because she guessed the green stuff wouldn't be enough to fill her up. She was constantly hungry at the moment, and she found if she didn't eat regularly and only stuck to vegetables and fruit with the odd bit of protein to go with it, she'd begin to feel sick. Touch wood – she tapped the wooden table with her fingers – she hadn't been sick since the incident in the bathroom, which she was putting down to the bath being too hot.

'I think I'll have a steak and fries, with all the trimmings,' Max announced, closing his menu and replacing it in the holder.

'I'd hardly class that as a quick bite,' she said. 'It'll take ages to cook.'

'Not if I have it rare,' he responded, and she blanched.

Rare meat had never been a favourite of hers, and today the thought of it made her a little queasy. She'd simply have to keep her eyes on her own plate and not look at his, she decided.

'How long have you worked at the Webber Corporation?' he asked as they waited for their food to arrive.

'Nearly twenty years,' she replied, taking a sip of water with a twist of lime. Max had ordered the same.

'It's a long time with the same company,' he observed.

It most certainly was, and if she had her time over again she would have left years ago. However, she had invested too much to leave now, especially when the top job was within sniffing distance.

'How about you?' she asked.

He gave her an amused look. 'About a week.'

'That's not what I meant. What made you want to come and work at the Webber Corporation?' It was a long shot, but she was hoping he might admit he was as ambitious as she suspected he was.

'Ricky made me an offer I couldn't refuse.'

She bet he did, she thought sourly.

'Why do you think he gave us joint custody of the Field Mouse Project?'

'I guess he wanted to see what I can do, but didn't want to let me loose on something so important until he knows I'm fully on board.'

'Wrong answer. The Pitbull would never have employed you if he didn't know what you are capable of. He doesn't take those kinds of risks; only financial ones.'

Max shrugged, then leant to the side slightly as a server placed his meal in front of him. 'Got any tomato ketchup?' he asked the waitress.

'Philistine,' Cynthia muttered.

'I happen to like tomato ketchup.'

'You have a finely cooked, if somewhat underdone steak on your plate and you're smothering it in red sauce.'

'Only the chips.'

Cynthia shook her head in despair. Max Oakland certainly wasn't pretentious. He appeared to know what he wanted and didn't give two hoots whether anyone else approved or not. She kind of respected that. Liked it, even. It was refreshing. It also told her he probably was the same when it came to business, and she filed the knowledge away for future reference.

She watched as he squirted the red stuff neatly on the side of his plate, speared a chip and dunked it in the blob of sauce.

'Mmm. Want one?' he offered.

Cynthia was sorely tempted. 'No thanks, I'm fine with my salad.'

'OK, but if you change your mind you'd better get in there fast – these little beauties aren't going to be around for long.' He ate another.

Cynthia placed a forkful of baby greens in her mouth and chewed. Darn it, she'd sell her soul for a chip right now.

As he concentrated on his food, Cynthia tried not to concentrate on him. After a week together she had discovered a little more about him. For instance, she knew he was forty-five, and he looked as though he took care of himself. The silver streaking his temples gave him some gravitas, counterbalancing the lack of lines on his forehead or around his mouth. His eyes had a couple of crow's feet though, and they crinkled at the corners when he smiled. It was his birthday in a couple of weeks, and she knew the date and his age because she'd looked him up on the HR database. But she didn't know much else. The database was surprisingly bare, with not much more than basic information. It didn't tell her where he'd worked in the past or anything else about the man, but she intended to find out and this lunch was the starting point.

The rest of the meal passed innocuously, both of them studiously avoiding talking about the project, the company, or any of their colleagues, unless it was in a general way, and Cynthia was careful not to disclose too much when it came to her opinion of people.

They did, however, discover they both had a love of cheesy eighties music and dark incomprehensible thrillers on Sky Atlantic, which they discussed for a while.

Max was quite good fun to talk to, she decided. It was just a pity the pair of them were professional rivals, and she warned herself not to get too close or to let her guard down.

If he'd been a lawyer, say, or a banker, or anything other than the man who was potentially after the same job as her, she might have considered…

But there was the little matter of her pregnancy to take into account, and it had been thoughts like the ones she was trying not to have about Max that had got her into the situation she was in.

It was only later, when she was sniffing her freshly laundered sheets and smoothing her hand across the 500 count thread as she slipped into bed, that she realised Max hadn't fully explained why Ricky had wanted them to work together, and she wondered what Max had meant when he'd said Ricky didn't think he was fully on board.

Why wouldn't he be? He'd just been made a director, so what wasn't Max Oakland not on board about? And if Ricky had wanted to see what Max was capable of, why hadn't he simply given him the project and let him make a success of it or not, as the case may be.

Something didn't feel right, but Cynthia had no idea what it was.

Chapter 6

She was going to be late, but there was absolutely nothing she could do about it. Taking another slug of water from the bottle she was clutching, she hurried out of the taxi and dashed through the open doors of the hospital, searching for directions. This place was a bloomin' maze, but at least she'd found an information board with coloured lines on it which were supposed to represent the coloured tape on the floor leading to the various departments.

When she saw the colour for the ante-natal department, she had to bite her lip to stop herself from singing *Follow the Yellow Brick Road*. She also had an urge to slip her arm through that of the nearest person and skip along the line.

Wondering if she was starting to unravel mentally, she pulled herself together and dutifully trotted down the corridor, following the line until she reached the check-in desk for the antenatal department.

The reception area was crowded with women in various stages of pregnancy, together with their husbands, partners, mothers, or friends.

Cynthia appeared to be the only mum-to-be who was on her own, and it made her a little… not sad, exactly… She didn't have the words to describe how she felt, so she concentrated on the increasing pressure in her bladder and how much she desperately needed the loo.

Big mistake. Now that she'd thought about her waterworks, it was the only thing she *could* think about. Drink at least half a litre of water the letter had told her, and she'd obediently done as she was told. Now though, she was regretting being quite so strict at adhering to the advice, and she began to squirm in her seat. If they didn't hurry up, she was in danger of having an accident and—

'Miss Smart? Sorry to keep you. Would you like to follow me?' The nurse waited for her to get slowly to her feet (any sudden moves might end in disaster) and showed her into a darkened room with a man sitting at a machine with a keyboard and monitor.

'This is Ed, he's your sonographer today,' the nurse explained, handing the man a folder. Cynthia caught a glimpse of a label on the outside with her name on it. 'Let me just check a few details, then you can pop on the bed, and pull your skirt down and lift your top up.'

Cynthia did as she was instructed, suddenly feeling unaccountably nervous. She was so far out of her comfort zone she might as well be on another planet. She'd never attended hospital before – heck, she hardly ever went to the GP – and she felt at a distinct disadvantage.

The only consolation she could find was that these people were professionals and no matter how new this was for her, they did this kind of thing day in, day out. She had to put her trust in them, so she lay back and took a deep breath.

'I'm just going to put this on you to protect your clothes,' the stenographer said, stuffing a large sheet of paper towel into her lowered waistband and another around the blouse where she'd tucked it into the bottom of her bra. 'The gel might feel cold,' he told her, 'but it's essential, I'm afraid.'

Cynthia almost shrieked when cold gel was smeared across her warm tummy and she curled her hands into fists as the sonographer pressed down.

'Let me know if it gets uncomfortable,' he advised, and she almost told him to stop right there before she wet herself.

He was staring intently at the screen and she focused on his face, which was eerily lit by the monitor, and suddenly her heart was in her mouth as she wondered what he could see and if everything was all right.

'I'll just take a few measurements,' he said after several long, long minutes, 'then I'll turn the screen around.'

'Is it OK? Is my baby—?' The word caught in her throat and she cleared it noisily. What on earth was the matter with her?

'Baby is fine. I'm dating him or her at thirteen weeks. Is that about right?'

'Yes.'

'Good, that ties in with the date of your last period. Just a minute…' He moved the wand across her lower abdomen, pressing down on her bladder and making her wince, and she prayed for it to soon be over.

She was desperate for the loo, and as soon as she was done here she had to get back to the office because she had a meeting with St—

'Oh…' she breathed as the sonographer turned the screen around and she saw a grainy black and white image.

Was that a head?

It was!

Cynthia could clearly see her baby's head on the monitor, and it was the most beautiful thing in the world.

Her baby. *Hers*!

The sonographer was pointing out the baby's legs and arms, and she had a body, too, and a nose and everything! Cynthia felt like crying. There was this whole new person growing inside her and for the first time since she'd peed on the stick, her baby seemed real. Not an abstract concept, not a word on a piece of plastic, not three missed periods, or swollen boobs, or vomit over the bathroom floor.

On the screen was her child. She was real and alive, and absolutely gorgeous even if it was difficult to tell exactly which bit of her was which as she squirmed around in the warm darkness.

Tears pricked Cynthia's eyes, and one of them escaped to trickle into her hair.

She was going to be a mother to this little scrap of humanity and without warning she felt such a rush of love and protectiveness it made her gasp. She couldn't wait to meet her.

'Can you tell me if it's a girl?' she asked. 'I'm sure it is, but I just need to check.'

'Sorry, no. You might be told at your twenty-week scan if there's a good enough image of the genital area. Right, your due date is estimated to be 30ᵗʰ November,' he told her, 'and we're done. As soon as you're ready, you can pop to the loo, then make your way back to the waiting area for your appointment with the antenatal team. Your scan photo will be ready in a few minutes, too.'

Cynthia muttered her thanks, wiped her sticky tummy, and tucked her skirt into her blouse, feeling like she was in a daydream. None of this seemed real. The only thing that didn't seem dreamlike was her baby.

That was very real indeed. Maybe the only real thing in her life – and certainly the only thing that truly mattered.

Chapter 7

Cynthia didn't care if she was late for her meeting. She didn't care if she never went to it at all. All she was interested in was the pretty little dresses, tiny socks, and minuscule bonnets in the display window.

Although how she came to be outside Petals and Pearls in the first place, she had little idea.

She remembered meeting one of the midwives, Marnie, who was friendly and incredibly nice, but not the midwife who'd been assigned to her because she was on annual leave, and she remembered being asked loads of questions – the trickiest one was about the baby's father, which she answered in only the vaguest of terms, because, let's face it, she didn't know his surname, let alone his medical history. She vividly recalled being measured, prodded, poked and weighed; she also remembered being given loads of leaflets and information sheets, which she had stuffed into her bag, being careful not to squash the precious scan photo. She was in a taxi and on her way back to work when she'd abruptly told the cab driver to pull over.

The next thing she knew, she was peering through a shop window and cooing over itty-bitty baby things.

Unable to stop herself, she pushed open the door and went inside.

She didn't have any intention of buying anything yet – it was much too soon for that – but she could browse, couldn't she?

Oh, my God, just look at that little dress with the matching frilly knickers, socks and headband. And what about that blanket!

Cynthia picked it up and held it against her cheek. It was the softest thing in the world, and she simply had to have it.

It wouldn't hurt to buy this one item, would it? It wasn't as though she was buying a cot or a pram or— Did babies honestly need a contraption to hang from a doorframe and bounce in, like tiny Olympic gymnasts, she questioned, spying just such a thing on the next shelf. Oh, but babies did need a butterfly mobile in the most wonderful pastel colours, and they very definitely needed a cuddly rabbit.

So she bought them.

She did have enough sense to ask if the shop could find a less conspicuous bag to put her purchases in though, and the lady behind the counter was obliging enough to send an assistant to the milliner's shop next door to ask them for one of their carrier bags. And by the time all that had been done and she'd flagged a taxi down, it was gone lunchtime and she'd totally missed her meeting.

As the euphoria of the morning seeped away, Cynthia slowly began to refocus on her job. The nearer she got to the office, the more surreal the past few hours were becoming. If it weren't for the photo in her bag, she might have thought she'd imagined the whole thing. Even the shopping part seemed like she'd been buying a baby shower gift for a friend or colleague, and she couldn't understand the compulsion that had made her buy the items in the first place. It wasn't like her to be so impulsive. She was a planner and a list writer, and she didn't even know if her baby would need, or even like, a butterfly mobile.

Just before the taxi drew up outside her office building, she took the leaflets and information sheets out of her handbag and stuffed them underneath the tissue-wrapped blanket. They'd be safe enough there; she'd look at them later when she got home.

For now, the only thing she wanted easy access to was the scan photo, so she put it in the front pocket of her handbag, and slipped the handles of the milliner's bag over her arm. Holding her head high, she walked into the foyer towards the lift. She'd make her apologies to Stephen – or rather, she'd ask Sally to do it for her – and arrange another time and date to meet with him. And in future, she'd allocate longer for all subsequent antenatal appointments just in case she was overtaken by another urge to fondle gorgeously soft baby items.

'There you are!' Sally cried as Cynthia entered her office. 'Mr Webber has been asking for you, Max Oakland wants to know if he can pop in and see you for a few minutes, and Stephen Landrigan says he was supposed to have a meeting with you but you didn't show. I checked your diary and he was definitely scheduled for today.' She stopped talking as her eyes went to the bag Cynthia was easing off her arm and trying to furtively slide under her desk.

'Get Ricky for me, would you?' Cynthia asked, ignoring her secretary's curiosity. 'And after you've done that, give my apologies to Stephen and rearrange. You can pencil Max in for two-thirty.'

'I did try calling you, but your phone was off or something,' Sally said. She looked rather anxious, her fingers playing with the necklace she always wore, and Cynthia could guess the reason, because she'd never gone AWOL before. She was always, always contactable, except when she was on a phone call or in a meeting. Yet today, she'd not only missed a meeting, but she'd switched her phone off. It was so unlike her that Sally must be finding it extremely disconcerting, and Cynthia felt she owed her personal assistant an explanation. Just not the true one...

'I, um, had something to sort out at the last minute,' she said. 'Nothing important.' Even as she said the words, she realised how silly they sounded – as though she'd ever go off grid and also miss a meeting for something that wasn't important. 'You couldn't make me a cup of tea, could you?'

Sally gave her a sharp look. 'Not coffee?'

'I fancy an Earl Grey.'

'Right.' Another sharp look.

Cynthia slipped off her jacket and hung it over the back of her chair. She never felt comfortable wearing it, but it was the done thing to have the corporate look going on. Suits for men, and suits for women. Thank God she didn't have to wear a tie, but the relief was counterbalanced by having to wear heels. Flats with a pencil skirt didn't look right somehow. At this very moment though, her feet were aching, so she sank into her chair, eased her shoes off, and let out a sigh.

45

Then she caught Sally watching her.

'What?' she asked.

'Nothing. I'll go make the tea. Milk? Sugar?'

'Just milk please, and have you got any biscuits?'

Her PA did a double take. 'I'm sorry, I thought you asked for biscuits.'

'I did.'

She could murder something sweet and stodgy, like sponge pudding and custard, but a biscuit would have to do. That was a blast from the past – her mum used to make a yummy sponge pudding. Speaking of which, it was time she paid her a visit and gave her the news. After all these years, her mother would be shocked to be told she was going to be a grandma. Cynthia hoped she'd be happy for her.

She'd best call her now, before the rest of the day ran away with her and she ended up not doing it at all, so she slipped her fingers into the front pocket of her handbag and pulled out her mobile. Her mum only ever answered numbers she recognised and no matter how many times Cynthia reminded her of the office number, her mum never picked up when she called her from it. She'd have to use her mobile phone, which was annoying because the signal could be a bit sketchy at times when she was in her office. She blamed the steel and concrete structure hidden beneath the walls' pale grey paint.

Sally was shaking her head slightly, looking confused, and Cynthia waited for her to leave before she dialled her mother's number.

'Mum, it's me.' She swivelled around in her chair and gazed out of the window, the sun glinting off the windows of the building opposite and making her squint. She loved that she had a decent view from her office – although the one from the

46

floor above where Ricky had his suite was even better again.

'Cynthia! How lovely.' Then a momentary pause, followed by, 'What's wrong? Is something the matter? It's not like you to phone in the middle of the day.'

'Nothing's wrong. I just wondered if you were free on Sunday.' Her mother had a far more active social life than Cynthia had ever had. If she wasn't at bingo, she was doing something with one of her church groups, or baking cakes for the WI, or reading to the residents of the nursing home down the road.

'I can be. I was going to visit the nursing home because they've got a craft day planned, but there'll be plenty of people there so they won't miss me. Why?'

'Can I pop round?' Travelling sixty odd miles from London to the little village outside Chichester where her mother lived could hardly be classed as "popping round".

'I knew it!' her mum declared. 'There's something wrong.'

'Not really. At least I hope not. I thought there was at first, but now I don't, and after today there most definitely isn't anything wrong.'

'You've lost me. What are you talking about? And if there's nothing wrong why can't you tell me now? You can't do this to me, darling.'

Cynthia smiled. 'I'll tell you when I get there. Will noon be OK?'

'Of course. I usually cook a roast,' her mum added, 'because Mr Williams next door doesn't look after himself since Iris died, so I take him a meal. Oh, and I always put a lunch up for Cate down the road, since she was diagnosed with cancer. But I can make you something else if you prefer?'

'A roast will be perfect.' She couldn't remember the last

time she'd eaten fluffy roast potatoes or a crispy Yorkshire pud.

There was a brief silence. 'Are you sure there's nothing wrong?' her mother asked, and Cynthia could hear the uncertainty and worry in her voice.

'I'm sure. I'll see you on Sunday.' She turned away from the window as she ended the call, then froze.

Sally had placed a cup of tea on the end of the desk and was standing there holding the picture Cynthia had been given at the hospital, growing understanding spreading across her face.

Cynthia's initial reaction was to deny all knowledge, or to lie.

Her second was to realise denial would be futile because Sally had joined up all the dots and the evidence was conclusive, with or without the scan photo.

'I'm sorry, this was on the floor next to your bag. I didn't mean to look, but… You're *pregnant*,' Sally blurted. 'I guessed you might be.'

'You can't tell anyone,' Cynthia urged. 'Please. Not yet.'

Sally handed her the picture and stepped in for a hug. 'Congratulations!'

Awkwardly Cynthia hugged her back. She'd never been a hugger and she didn't think she'd ever had any physical contact with Sally in all the years they'd been working together. Nevertheless, she appreciated the sentiment.

'I won't, I promise,' Sally vowed, releasing her and stepping back. 'How far gone are you? You must be thrilled.'

'Thirteen weeks, but no one can know about it,' she repeated.

'They won't hear it from me,' Sally assured her. 'But you do need to let HR know soon, because you'll be entitled to time

48

off for antenatal appointments, and in a few weeks you'll need to give them your MAT B1 form so they can—'

'My *what?*'

'Didn't they tell you all this at the antenatal clinic? That *is* where you've been this morning, isn't it?' Sally gave the bag with the milliner's logo and name on it a pointed stare.

Not for one second did her personal assistant believe she'd bunked off a meeting with Stephen Landrigan in order to buy a hat. How would Sally react if she knew what was really in the bag?

'Nothing gets past you,' Cynthia observed, wryly. 'They probably did, but I was in shock and I wasn't listening. They did give me a load of leaflets, so the information is probably in there somewhere. I'll go through it all when I get home.'

Sally's expression became serious. 'Mr Webber can't sack you, you know, if that's what you're worried about.'

'I know. But you've seen the figures. There's not one woman who has a family who is higher than a mid-level manager. And the only other woman sitting on the board has kids who are all grown up. The Pitbull doesn't think women with children below the age of eighteen can offer the company the same level of commitment as women without.'

'Maybe they don't want to,' Sally suggested. 'I wouldn't want your job for all the tea in China, and my children are in university now and don't need me so much. I couldn't begin to imagine doing what you do and trying to raise a family at the same time.'

'But I'm going to have to if I want…' She trailed off. She hadn't shared her ambition with anyone, not even Sally.

Her secretary gave her a measured look. 'You might think you know what you want right now, but that may change when the baby is born,' she warned. 'All I can say is, they're not babies for long, and if you spend every waking hour in work you'll miss things you can never get back. Anyway.' She walked towards the door. 'That's only my opinion, and I've every faith you'll do what's best for you and your little one.'

It was only when the door closed softly behind her, did Cynthia realise Sally hadn't once asked about the baby's father.

Chapter 8

Cynthia breathed the fresh air, smelling the scent of newly mown grass, and watched the scenery unfold as green field after green field rolled by, separated by miles of hedgerows. She caught the sound of birds chirping, the bleat of woolly sheep, and the rumble of a tractor engine – all so very different from the sights, smells and noises of the city.

She had the car's soft top down, and was enjoying the feel of the wind ruffling her hair and the open road beneath the wheels. It was a joy to drive the BMW along relatively traffic-free roads, and for a second she thought she should have been satisfied with the car and not had a second midlife crisis in California.

But then, she'd never have become pregnant, would she? And that would simply be unthinkable now, because this baby was very wanted indeed since she'd seen it on the monitor. She would probably have to part-ex the car though.

'You're looking well!' her mum exclaimed as she swooped in for a hug as soon as Cynthia unfolded herself from the car, and she allowed herself to be pressed into her mother's arms. The scent of Estée Lauder filled her nose and she inhaled deeply, the familiar perfume soothing her.

Unusually, it was Maggie who pulled away first, holding Cynthia at arm's length and searching her face for clues as to what might be wrong with her daughter.

'I feel well,' Cynthia said with a smile. If she ignored her sore boobs, the on-off nausea, and the fatigue which caught her unawares. From what she'd read, she should be past all this, but she guessed that now she knew she was pregnant, her body was making up for lost time and cramming them all in now, because she'd not experienced any of those tell-tale signs before she'd taken the pregnancy test.

'Let's get you inside, then you can tell me all about it,' her mum said, linking arms with her and walking her along the cobbled path to the front door of the little cottage.

'I'll put the kettle on. Lunch won't be ready for another hour or so,' Maggie said, as Cynthia gazed around the kitchen she knew so well and which hadn't changed a bit over the years, except for a new fridge and the addition of a canary yellow microwave.

The aroma of roasting beef made her mouth water, and she was looking forward to lunch already.

Hunger gnawing at her, she raided the old biscuit barrel next to the kettle and helped herself to a handful of custard creams from the scratched and chipped tin, ignoring her mother's raised eyebrows.

'Coffee?' her mum asked.

'Tea, please.'

The eyebrows went up another notch. 'Now then, are you going to tell me, or do I have to beat it out of you with a bourbon?'

Cynthia waited until her mum was sitting down at the kitchen table and they both had a mug in front of them before she announced, 'I'm pregnant.'

Her mother froze.

'Did you hear what I said?' Cynthia asked.

Her mum nodded but didn't say anything. Her eyes were out on stalks, her mouth had dropped open, and her complexion had suddenly paled.

Cynthia's heart dropped to her ballet pumps. 'Are you terribly upset?'

Maggie shook her head. 'I… um… gosh! That's the last thing I expected to hear. I thought you were going to tell me you'd been promoted.' Her eyes filled with tears.

'Aw, Mum.' Cynthia felt a tell-tale prickling behind her eyes, and she fanned her face with her hands. 'Please don't be disappointed.'

'My dear girl, what on earth makes you think I'm disappointed? I'm thrilled.' And with that she burst into tears.

Cynthia got to her feet and went over to her mother, wrapping her arms around her, tears trickling down her own cheeks. She felt ridiculous. She never cried, and this wasn't exactly the worst thing in the world to happen. Now she'd had time to get used to the idea, she was pleased about it. She'd thought her chances of being a mother had long gone.

'I never thought I'd be a granny,' her mum sniffed. 'What took you so long?'

Cynthia hugged her tighter. It wasn't as though this pregnancy was planned, and for the last few years the thought of marriage and motherhood hadn't crossed her mind.

'How many weeks are you? When did you find out? Have you had a scan yet? When will I get to meet the father? Ooh, I'm thrilled to bits!' Her mother squeezed her hands into fists and shook them in her excitement.

'One at a time, Mum. I'm fourteen weeks, I only found out two weeks ago, and you're the first person I've told.' Sally didn't count because her personal assistant hadn't been told – she'd guessed. 'Here.' Cynthia retrieved the scan photo from her bag and handed it to her mum.

'Oh, my, would you look at that. Hello, baby.' Maggie stroked the picture with her fingertip and sniffed again. 'That's so precious.'

'You can keep it; I've scanned it into my phone.'

'Wait until I tell the girls,' she cried, and Cynthia smiled. "The girls" consisted of her mum's large circle of friends, none of them younger than sixty.

Her mum could finally join in with the stories of grandchildren and pregnant daughters and daughters-in-law, although by now, many of "the girls" were at the great-grandma stage. Cynthia and her mum were a bit late to the party.

'What's his name?' her mum asked.

Cynthia blinked. 'Do you think it's a boy?' she asked, thoughtfully. 'I've got a feeling it's a girl, but I haven't got as far as thinking of names yet.'

'I was talking about the baby's father.'

'Ah.'

Her mother gave her a shrewd look. 'I take it from your reaction he's no longer around?'

'No…'

'I hope he's going to accept his responsibilities, even if the two of you aren't together. A child needs its father, even if you don't need the financial help.'

'He doesn't know.'

Maggie carefully put the photo down on the table. 'Cynthia, you have to tell him. He has a right to know.'

How on earth was she going to explain to her elderly mother that she'd had a one-night stand and had no clue as to Stan's surname or even which country he currently lived in. Shame and regret, hot and heavy, weighed her down and her shoulders slumped. She didn't make a habit of jumping into bed with complete strangers. She didn't make a habit of sleeping with anyone at all, however long she'd known them, and the last time she'd had a date was a couple of years ago. There never seemed to be the time. So when she'd unexpectedly had some time on her hands and gorgeous Stan had made it clear he'd found her as attractive as she'd found him, then…

Cynthia had read enough since she'd discovered she was pregnant to guess her sudden lust and loss of inhibitions had been as much to do with her hormones having one last desperate attempt to procreate, as it had been the result of a sun-drenched day on the beach and a star-filled night, and the knowledge that only she would ever be aware of her indiscretion.

Hah! The gods were having a good laugh at her expense.

'I can't tell him,' she said to her mother.

Maggie blew out her cheeks. 'Is he married? Is that it?'

No, but it would do as an explanation.

When she failed to say anything further, her mother sighed. 'How are you going to manage?'

'I'll be fine. I'm going to employ a nanny of some sort – I haven't looked into it in depth yet, and I'll have to change the car.'

'That's your plan for coping with a baby, is it? You're going to keep on working as though nothing's happened, and swap your fancy car for a Range Rover.'

'Of course not! Yes, I'm going to keep on working, but I know I'll have to make a few adjustments.'

'More than a few,' her mother muttered. 'Especially if you haven't got a partner to help.'

'I don't need a partner. Thousands of women have babies and go back to work.'

'I wonder how many of those who do go back to work, do so because they have no choice?'

'Well, I want to, OK? I enjoy my job and I've worked damned hard to get to where I am now.'

'Babies don't care about your job, or how hard you work. They just want their mums to be there.'

'I will be there!' Cynthia protested. She *knew* she shouldn't have told her mother – she might have guessed she'd try to put obstacles in her way. This was the very reason she couldn't wait to leave Little Milling when she was younger.

'Will you?' Maggie asked. 'Or will it be the nanny who'll be there when your baby is teething and wants its mum. Or to take him or her to playgroup, or watch him take his first steps? I'm just going to say one thing and then I'll shut up – you can't have it all. You might think you can, but when you're in work you'll be worrying about the baby and wondering what you're missing. You'll feel incredibly guilty, too. And when you're at home because the baby is ill and won't settle for anyone else, you'll feel guilty because you should be at work. Even when you are there, you'll be wishing you were at home with your child. And don't start me off on how tired you'll feel.'

Maggie paused for breath and Cynthia jumped in. 'Thanks, Mum, but I'll be fine. I can cope with a bit of tiredness. Besides, looking after a baby isn't an illness. I'll manage.'

'All I'm saying is, think seriously about it. And if you'd like me to come and stay with you for the first few weeks – longer, if needs be – then I will. The offer is there.'

Cynthia stretched out a hand and covered her mother's. 'I appreciate it, but you'll hate it in the city.'

'How about you come to stay with me, instead? Not permanently, although you're welcome to do exactly that, if you want to – you know I'd love to have you – but while you're on maternity leave.'

Cynthia was taken aback. A couple of weeks at the cottage, being looked after by her mum, sounded idyllic but it was hardly worth it. She'd be back in London before she knew it, and trying to get into a new routine. No, she might as well stay in her apartment and start as she meant to go on.

She realised her mother was desperate to see as much of her grandchild as she could, but it would be easier for her to come to London, rather than for Cynthia to come here. Maybe she'd suggest it nearer the date.

But as she watched her mum pottering in the well-worn kitchen, Cynthia imagined a small child sitting in the middle of the floor and playing with pots and pans, much as she herself had done when she was little. And that was far easier than picturing her daughter in her own incredibly neat and pristine apartment.

The baby would love her mother's garden, too – the rope swing in the apple tree down the bottom, the hammock strung in the corner, the cat sunning itself in the middle of the flower bed. She could see it now…

Cynthia shook herself. Children grew up in apartments in the city all the time, and it didn't do them any harm. Besides, her job was there, her life was there, and her future was there. Having a baby shouldn't make the slightest bit of difference.

It was only when she was driving back to London on the busy A roads, feeling mentally and physically exhausted, that the doubts her mother had planted resurfaced.

'I'll be fine,' she muttered aloud. '*We'll* be fine.' And she firmly pushed them to the back of her mind because things were different now to when her mother was carrying her. Women these days *could* have it all. Couldn't they?

Chapter 9

Cynthia massaged her right temple and squinted at the screen. Max had a PowerPoint presentation on it and Jon Everton had been grilling him very thoroughly about it. Now and again she did think the shoe should be on the other foot and *they* should be asking the Chief Exec of Field Hotels the searching questions, not the other way around. After all, Ricky's company was the one putting up the collateral and taking the financial hit. Anyone would think the Field Hotels chain were at the top of their game, when in fact they were struggling to get out of the fourth division.

The past two weeks had been intense, with more early starts and late nights than normal, and she was exhausted. Yet they weren't any nearer to coming to an agreement with Field Hotels than when Ricky had handed her and Max the project a month ago.

Max gave her a questioning look, and Cynthia let her hand drop to the table and tried to pretend she didn't have a headache, she wasn't so tired she could easily fall asleep there and then, and she didn't need to go to the loo for the third time in an hour. She was also starving hungry (when wasn't she?) had backache, and longed to go home. It was nearly eight in the evening, and she'd been up and at it since six that morning. She was *knackered*, for pity' sake.

Thank goodness for Max. She hated to admit it, but he'd been a godsend, shouldering more than his share of the burden. Of course, she let him think she was testing him. Or giving him enough rope to hang himself. It didn't matter which, just as long as he didn't guess the real reason – that she was struggling, both physically and mentally. She could almost cope with the physical stuff being pregnant was throwing at her, but as the weeks went on she found she was becoming more and more woolly headed. And it terrified her. Baby brain was *a thing*, apparently, and she seemed to have it in abundance.

'The share prices are dropping month on month,' Max was saying. 'Cynthia, do you have the percentage comparison for this time last year?' He asked this of her knowing full well she had. They'd discussed it earlier before they went into the meeting. He was going to present the argument and she was going to back him up with cold, hard facts and figures.

Except… she couldn't for the life of her remember what that particular figure was. 'Erm, I have it here; just a second.' She scrabbled around on her iPad for a couple of embarrassingly long seconds before she found what she wanted. In a daze, she read the figure out, nausea roiling in her stomach. She was losing it, seriously losing it, and she realised she was perilously close to tears.

Shocked, because she never cried, she took a deep breath and gritted her teeth.

'I think we're done for this evening, don't you?' she announced. 'Jon, you have everything you need to take back to your board. I don't expect a decision tomorrow, or even next week, but I do expect one shortly.'

She climbed to her feet, her palms resting flat on the tabletop as she levered herself up. Her back was in half, and there was a dull ache across the lower part of her tummy, similar to a period pain.

Max didn't flinch at her abrupt closure of the meeting. He clicked out of the PowerPoint and closed his laptop with a snap, as if this had been previously agreed on.

Jon was nodding slowly. 'I can't promise a definite decision by the end of next week, but it will allow us to open the negotiation box. It was nice meeting you Ms Smart, and you too, Max.'

As she and Max left the room, it didn't go unnoticed that the chief exec of Field Hotels had been far less formal with Max than he had with her. It was almost as though he knew him.

A wave of dizziness crashed over her, and Cynthia put out a hand to steady herself. The wall of the corridor was cool under her palm and she had an urge to rest her hot forehead against it.

'Are you all right?' Max's hand was on her elbow, his voice in her ear.

'I just need some air, that's all.' What she wanted was to lie down, but they were at Field Hotel's head office, a good forty-minute drive across town from her apartment. It would probably be quicker to walk, but she didn't think she could manage it, despite her craving for air. It had been horribly stuffy in there. Had the chain never heard of air-con? No wonder the company was going under if they treated their paying guests the same way as their staff.

Max kept close to her side as they waited for the lift, and quickly ushered her inside when it arrived, his expression one of concern. She leant against the back wall, studiously ignoring her reflection in the mirrored sides (why did companies do that?), not wanting to see the paleness of her face or the bags under her eyes.

When it shuddered to a halt and the doors pinged open, she noticed a sign for the ladies' toilet and she made a beeline for it, calling, 'I'll only be a sec,' over her shoulder, hoping she'd make it in time, because the urge to go had suddenly increased to unbearable proportions.

Crikey, she thought – she knew drinking copious amounts of water was good for her, but if this was the result, she'd stick to just a couple of glasses a day in future.

She barged into a cubicle, yanked her skirt up and her knickers down and…

The resulting trickle was disappointing when she'd been anticipating a flood. Yet when she thought she'd finished, the urge to go was still strong and the ache in her lower abdomen had intensified. Her back was in bits too, and all she wanted to do was to curl up in bed with a hot water bottle. Ironic, because that was an item she didn't own and hadn't thought about since her mum used to give her one when she had period pains as a teenager.

Suddenly her heart froze.

There was a red stain on the toilet paper. Not much, but enough.

No, no, this couldn't be happening. Not when she had come to terms with being pregnant. Not when she had fallen in love with the image on the monitor. Not when she'd fallen in love with the little girl in the bath.

She tidied herself up, washed her hands, and bit back a sob.

'Keep it together,' she muttered, thankful there was no one else in the loos, and when she failed to take her own advice, she shoved her fist in her mouth to stop herself from falling apart completely.

She wasn't sure how long she stayed that way, biting down on her knuckles, her face a mask of pain in the mirror, but she gradually came to her senses, realising she had to make a move.

Splashing water on her face, she resisted the urge to return to the cubicle to see whether there was any more blood. There would be time enough to check when she got home and had some privacy. In the back of her mind she was hoping she'd imagined it, but her heart knew the truth and it scared her more than she'd ever been scared in her life.

She wanted this baby, goddammit! This was her last chance. She'd thought motherhood had passed her by and it hadn't bothered her before, but now she'd been given a chance. And it was about to be taken away.

Max was waiting for her as she emerged from the ladies' loos. He was leaning against one of the pillars, his attention on his phone, but he glanced up at her as she approached.

'What the hell…? What's wrong?' he demanded, slipping the phone into his pocket and stepping forwards to catch hold of her arm.

His touch was comforting, but she shook him off. 'I'm fine.'

'You don't look it.'

'Thanks.' She was aiming for sarcastic, but instead she sounded hurt. And frightened.

'Are you ill? Can I do anything to help?' The kindness in his voice was her undoing and she burst into tears.

'Here, sit down.' He guided her to one of the squishy seats in the reception area and sat her down, then handed her a tissue out of a small pack he took from his pocket. 'Do you want to tell me what's wrong?'

She most certainly did not, but she felt so awful, hot yet chilled, aching and shaky, and she needed to go to the toilet yet again. She knew she had to have help, and the last thing she wanted was to lose her baby in what amounted to a public toilet. And if there was any chance of saving her – any chance at all – then she had to take it. Which meant going to the hospital right now.

'I need to go to the hospital,' she said.

Max didn't hesitate. He didn't question and he didn't argue. He simply walked across the foyer, spoke to the receptionist on duty, then came back for her. Helping her to her feet (she leant on him far more than she wanted to) he led her outside just as a taxi drew up.

Opening the door for her, he made sure she was safely inside before he darted around to the other side and got in next to her, telling the driver to take them to the nearest hospital which had an Accident and Emergency department.

'You'll be fine,' he murmured, taking her cold hand in his. He was staring at her with concern, but his prompt and unquestioning handling of the situation made her hope he was right. She felt better for having him there, not so alone, not quite as scared as she would have been if she was by herself.

'How are you feeling?' he asked.

'Awful.'

'It's probably just a bug or something you ate.'

64

'I'm pregnant and I think I'm losing the baby,' she blurted, tears trickling down her face once more.

'Oh, hell.'

'Yeah.' Her laugh was small and bitter. "Oh, hell" just about summed it up.

'Driver, can you speed it up,' he called through the partition window. 'It's an emergency.' He turned back to Cynthia. 'Is there anyone I can call for you? Husband, partner?'

Her heart was full of despair as she said, 'There's no one,' and she looked out of the window so she didn't see the pity in his eyes. She did feel his arm slip around her though, and when he pulled her close she sank into his solidness, trying to draw some of his strength into her, because she had a feeling she might need it in the hours, days, and weeks ahead.

If she lost this baby, she would only have herself to blame.

Chapter 10

The sense of urgency coursing through her didn't seem to be reflected in the A&E reception staff as they took her details and told her to take a seat and wait until she was called.

'How long will that be?' she asked, her hands on her tummy as though she could keep her baby safe inside her by sheer force of will alone.

'Waiting time is currently just under three hours,' the woman behind the screen said, and Max drew her away before she could argue.

'I'm sure if they thought it was serious, you'd be seen straight away,' he said.

Cynthia wasn't sure that was the case at all. She suspected they dealt with miscarriages all the time, so hers wasn't anything special.

Except, to her it was. And she berated herself for not understanding just how special, until there was a possibility she might lose her baby.

Max sat close, his solid presence providing a modicum of comfort. He fetched her a hot cup of plastic-flavoured tea, kept her seat for her when she made her umpteenth trip to the loo, and held her hand when she returned tight-lipped and red-eyed.

He didn't say anything, he didn't need to. Having him there was enough. She dreaded to think how she'd have coped if she had been on her own. Which surprised her – she was confident, capable, and always sorted things out for herself. But this was something she had no experience of, and neither had she ever felt so out of control.

'Miss Smart?'

Cynthia jumped when she heard her name called and she scrambled to her feet. 'That's me.' She'd only taken a few steps towards the nurse who was holding a door open for her, when she realised Max wasn't behind her.

'Will you come with me?' she asked in a small voice, then hastened to add, 'You don't have to if you don't want to. And please don't feel obliged to wait for me; I can make my own way home.'

'I didn't think you'd want me with you,' he said, 'but if you're sure?'

She nodded and he followed her as she was led into a cubicle. It was empty but she was told to take a seat, so she sat, and Max sat down next to her. Her hand reached for his and gripped it tightly.

A young man swooped in and plonked himself down. 'I'm Doctor Keithly, one of the junior doctors. What seems to be the problem?'

She'd already told the lady on reception, but she repeated her story, this time in a little more detail, with an apologetic look at Max when she got to the bit about the blood on the loo paper, because he genuinely didn't need to hear that. He didn't seem bothered though, and she was grateful for his stoic attitude.

'OK, let's pop you on the bed and have a feel of your tummy,' the doctor said, and she obediently climbed onto the bed, after undoing the zip of her skirt and easing it down.

Max looked away, and she hoped it was to preserve her modesty and not because he was repulsed by the fact he was having to witness his colleague in a state of half undress.

The doctor rubbed his hands together and gently felt all around her tummy. Cynthia held her breath. His expression didn't change and when he straightened up and walked out of the cubicle, she let it out slowly, hanging onto her composure by a thread.

He returned with a nurse wheeling a machine on a stand, and said, 'Let's have a little listen.' And with that, he smeared some gel over her exposed stomach and pressed on it with a wand.

For a few moments all they could hear was a vague noise like listening to the ocean through a seashell, then the doctor moved the probe and suddenly the air was filled with the sound of an incredibly rapid whooshing noise.

'That's your baby's heartbeat,' the doctor told her. 'It's nice and strong, and the rate is about what we'd expect for your stage of pregnancy.'

Cynthia was mesmerised. It was the most wonderful sound she'd ever heard, and she felt she could listen to it all day. She turned to Max in awe, to see he had a wide smile on his face. She reached out and he scooted closer, giving her hand a reassuring squeeze.

'Oh, my,' she said. 'She's alive.'

'She most certainly is.' The doctor was smiling, too.

'Why the blood though? And why do I feel so awful?'

'I suspect you might have a UTI. I'll get a nurse to take your temperature and blood pressure, then if you could fill a specimen bottle for me, we can do a quick dip test.'

'You think I've got a water infection?'

'That's the most likely explanation, so we'll rule that out first.'

Max studiously peered through a gap in the cubicle curtain as she used a tissue to remove as much of the gel as possible and adjusted her skirt and top. It was only when she stood beside him that he looked at her. And the relief and tenderness she saw on his face made her feel a little dizzy.

The urine test confirmed the doctor's suspicion and Cynthia nearly sagged with relief. She still felt awful, but at least she knew the reason and that her baby wasn't in any danger.

'That's good news,' Max said, as they left the hospital, Cynthia clutching a paper bag containing antibiotics.

She was a little reluctant to take them, but the doctor assured her it was safe and that she'd have a bit of a job on her hands fighting off the bacterial infection without the tablets.

'How are you feeling? You must be exhausted.' Max's shoulder brushed hers as they walked, and she wished he'd hold her hand again. It had felt incredibly comforting.

'I am tired,' she confirmed. 'Relieved, too. I just want to go home and sleep for a week.'

'Take a tablet first,' he warned her. 'And I bet you've hardly eaten all day.'

She pulled a face. He was right. She'd had a sandwich at lunchtime, but nothing since and it was now gone midnight.

69

'It's too late to eat,' she protested.

'You'd better have something, even if it's just a piece of toast. No wonder you're ill if you don't look after yourself.' He sounded stern and she sent him a sheepish look.

'I wish I'd known you were pregnant,' he continued, jerking his head towards her hardly noticeable bump. 'I would have scheduled the meeting for a more suitable time.'

'You weren't to know, and I could always have said it wasn't convenient,' she argued. She still didn't feel too well, but she felt infinitely better than she had earlier when she thought she was losing her baby; better enough to argue back.

'We'll pick some food up on the way,' he said, and she raised her eyebrows. 'I'm not putting you in a taxi and sending you home on your own,' he told her. 'I'm coming with you to make sure you get there safely, and I'm also going to make sure you have something to eat. Now, what do you fancy? There are still a few places open.'

While she waited for the taxi to pull alongside, Cynthia thought. 'McDonald's,' she said, eventually, even though she'd normally baulk at the very idea of fast food. 'Big Mac, large fries, and a strawberry milkshake.' She would have loved to have a fizzy drink to go with it, but she was worried it might give her heartburn, so she'd have water. The doctor had told her to drink as much as she could to help flush the bugs out of her system, and water was the best thing. Wonderful; as if she didn't guzzle enough of the stuff already.

Max asked the cabbie to stop off at a drive-through on the way to her apartment, which he did, and shortly afterwards the pair of them were tucking into their food in her living room, Cynthia thinking it was ridiculous she could feel ill yet still feel incredibly hungry.

'Better?' he asked her after she'd stuffed the last of the fries into her mouth and had jammed a straw into the milkshake.

She nodded. 'I've still got an achy back and pains in my tummy, and I can't get warm, but at least I don't feel like throwing up anymore.'

'Good, it would be a waste of a Big Mac 'n' fries if you did.'

'Thank you for your help tonight,' she said, shyly. It was going to be hard to forge a working relationship going forward, and although she was incredibly grateful for him being there for her, she was also starting to feel extremely embarrassed. How was she supposed to look him in the eye in the morning when he'd seen her in such a state?

'It was nothing,' he said. 'Anyone would have done the same.'

An image of Ricky sprung to mind, and Cynthia knew her boss certainly wouldn't have. The most he would have done would be to call a taxi for her and shove her into it. Not personally, of course – he would have got one of his minions to do it for him.

'Thank you all the same. I don't know what I would have done without you there.' Her voice broke and tears were perilously close to the surface once more.

'There's no need to be upset,' he said, getting up and coming around to her side of the table and giving her a hug.

She snivelled into his chest, breathing in the scent of his cologne and him. It was a very comforting smell, but it also made her very conscious he was a man and she was a woman, and she hadn't been held so tenderly by anyone of the opposite sex for a very long time indeed. Stan didn't count – there had been nothing tender about their encounter.

'Let's get you into bed,' Max said, and despite feeling wretched, Cynthia snorted in amusement.

'I didn't mean—!'

She sniggered. 'I know. I was winding you up.'

'If you're well enough to wind me up, then you're well enough to see to yourself,' he retorted, then did the exact opposite by helping her get to her feet. 'Are you safe to be left on your own?' he asked. 'I can stay if you want. The couch will be fine.'

'No, you go. You've done enough and all I'm going to do is to turn the heating on and go to bed.' She gave him a gentle push towards the door. 'It's incredibly late, and we've got work in the—'

'No, you haven't,' he interrupted, and her mouth dropped open.

Blimey, he could be forceful when he wanted to be.

'You are not going into work tomorrow. In fact, I don't want to see you in for the rest of the week,' he said.

'You can't stop me.' She knew her bottom lip was jutting out because it always did when she was thwarted.

'No, I can't,' he agreed. 'But what I can do is tell Ricky the reason you're not at full throttle tomorrow. Because you won't be, you know. You might be feeling a tiny bit better, but not much.'

'He won't care if I've got a water infection. He'll expect me to be there regardless.'

'Even if he knows you're pregnant?'

'You wouldn't!'

'I would, and considering you're so keen for him not to know…?'

'That's blackmail.'

'Yep. It's also called being concerned.'

She knew he was right, and she was starting to feel decidedly unwell again; but that didn't mean she enjoyed being bossed around by him. 'If I must stay home, then I must,' she said. 'I'm not happy about it, though.'

'I don't care.'

But he did care, she realised – he cared about *her*. After he'd gone and she was tucked up in bed, her symptoms having subsided a little once more, she realised how comforting it was that he did.

Stupidly – because it would never happen – she wished he cared about her as a woman, and not because she was a fellow employee who happened to have fallen ill in his presence.

And her last thought before she dropped off to sleep, was to wonder why she wanted him to care at all.

Chapter 11

The following morning Cynthia was already awake and up when there was a knock at the door. She checked the time – six-thirty; far too early for it to be the postman or for any deliveries. And, apart from the odd takeaway – those were the only people who knocked on her door.

Her shock at seeing Max standing there, looking as if he'd had a full eight hours sleep and not the two or three she knew he'd had, must have shown in her face.

'Didn't expect to see me, did you?' he said, stalking past her and waving a bag of something delicious-smelling under her nose.

'What are you doing?' she demanded.

'Making sure you aren't about to do anything silly, like go into work, for instance. You look like crap, by the way.'

'Thank you.' She felt it, too. The sleep she had managed to snatch had been restless – her back and tummy still ached, she'd felt alternately too hot then chilled to the bone, and the

74

big muscles in her thighs were sore. Add a headache and gritty eyes to that little lot, and she didn't feel the best. 'Do I *look* as though I'm about to go to work?'

Fluffy jammies was a look, admittedly, but not one she intended sporting in the office anytime soon, and she needed a shower and to wash her hair. A bit of make-up wouldn't go amiss either, if she wasn't to scare small children.

However, she felt too tired and unwell to even brush her teeth.

Yet a part of her wished Max hadn't seen her looking so rough. Which must mean she was getting better, right?

Wrong.

The simple act of dragging herself out of bed and boiling the kettle had knackered her. The exhausting task of opening the door to him had worn her out even more.

She watched him waltz down the hall and into her kitchen, her eyes heavy, and she staggered after him on wooden legs.

'Croissants,' he announced, opening the bag. 'Do you want tea or coffee?'

'Tea.' Her throat was dry and despite drinking copious amounts of water throughout the night, she was thirsty. The sight of the pastries didn't do anything for her, though.

He popped the croissant on a plate, flicked the switch on the kettle, and poured her a glass of water. Handing it to her, he opened the tub of tablets and gave her one.

'Do you intend to supervise me whenever it's time to take my antibiotic?' she asked, gulping it down, then slumping into the nearest chair.

'If that's what it takes.'

'I'm perfectly capable of remembering to take a tablet. I don't need supervision.'

'But a bit of TLC wouldn't go amiss, would it? And I think you could do with some right now.'

She shrugged. 'I can manage.'

'I know, but you shouldn't have to "manage". Is the baby's father on the scene?'

Cynthia was taken aback. How dare he ask such a personal question? It was none of his business. The implied criticism in his voice didn't help her mood.

He noticed her outrage. 'I'm only asking because I care.'

'You do? Why?'

'Why not? It's the moral and human thing to do. I'm not in the habit of walking away when someone is in distress, especially when I can help.'

'That's very admirable of you.' Even unwell, she could throw out a bit of sarcasm.

'I don't care if you think I'm weak or soft, or just plain stupid. That's the way I am.'

'You'll need to toughen up and grow a thick skin if you want to follow in the Pitbull's footsteps.'

'Who says I do? I can't think of anything I'd rather do less.'

'Really?' She didn't believe him.

'Really. Now, here's your tea and don't forget to eat a croissant.'

'Aren't you having one?'

'I've got to get to the office.' He peered at her. 'I don't think you will, but just in case stupidity overrides common sense and you decide going into work is a good idea, remember what I said.'

'I'm surprised you haven't told him already.'

'You haven't got a very good opinion of me, have you? I'm not going to tell Ricky anything. Not unless you force me to.

I'm only looking out for you,' he added, as he walked out of the door.

And to her surprise, she discovered she believed him.

Chapter 12

'What are you doing here?' Cynthia asked, opening the door to Sally later that afternoon.

'I thought I'd stop by to check on you. You don't look well.'

That seemed to be a common consensus today, she thought, opening the door wider to let her personal assistant in.

Sally's eyes darted everywhere as Cynthia showed her into the living room, and Cynthia was conscious this was the first time her PA had visited her apartment. She was bound to be curious, but even so Cynthia found it a little disconcerting. She never had any visitors, and now she'd had two in less than twenty-four hours – one of them twice.

'I've brought you some supplies,' Sally said, gesturing to the carrier bag in her hand. 'Cranberry juice, Lucozade, milk, and bread in case you were running low.'

'Grapes?'

'Sorry, no. Did you want some? I can always run out—'

'I'm joking. It's just, that's what you give people in hospital, isn't it? I feel like an invalid.'

'You are, for the moment,' Sally retorted. 'And if you don't look after yourself properly, you definitely will be in hospital. Have you taken your antibiotic?'

'Not you, as well.' Cynthia frowned. 'What has Max told you?'

'Everything.'

'He was supposed to be keeping it quiet – he didn't know you already knew I am pregnant.' That was the last time she trusted him.

'Blame me. After you left a message to say you wouldn't be in today because you weren't well, I called him to let him know you couldn't make your nine a.m. meeting with him and he already knew you wouldn't be in. It took a bit of doing, but I winkled it out of him, and when he told me he'd accompanied you to the hospital, I knew he knew.'

'Did he send you?'

'I would have come anyway. I was worried about you. We both were.'

Cynthia's eyes prickled. Cross, she willed the threatened tears away. This was ridiculous – she wasn't a crier. But neither was she used to people worrying about her. Deciding to blame her reaction on the ridiculous pregnancy hormones, she changed the subject.

'How did Ricky take it when you told him I was off sick? I would have phoned him myself, but…' She felt guilty for landing the unwelcome task in Sally's lap, but she knew if she'd have spoken directly to her boss, she'd have ended up going into work. Then Max would have made good on his threat, and all hell would have broken loose – and she honestly hadn't felt up to it.

'He… er… doesn't know,' Sally replied, biting her lip and twiddling with the chain on the necklace she always wore. The twiddling was one of her tells – she did it when she was worried or nervous.

'What? Why not? I'll have to call him and—'

'There's no need. He's not been in the office all day, he's not phoned, and you've not had any emails from him.'

'That's as may be, but he still should be told I'm off work.'

'I'll do it tomorrow,' Sally promised. 'But I warn you, if he calls you at home, he'll have me to answer to. He can't harass staff who are off sick.'

'He can, and he will. And I'm not just staff. He expects a lot from his directors.'

'He gets it too, but he's got no right to demand blood,' Sally argued.

'It probably doesn't matter anyway. Not now,' she replied, morosely.

'Because you're pregnant? That's not on!'

'Because he's lining Max up as his replacement. It's obvious.'

'Oh, hon, I'm sure he's not. He wouldn't do that to you.'

Cynthia shot her an incredulous look.

'Yeah, OK, he would,' Sally conceded. 'But if Max knew what was going on, I'm sure he wouldn't be happy about it.'

Bless her, Sally could be so naïve at times.

'Max Oakland didn't get to be a director of a company the size of this one, if he didn't have a ruthless streak in him,' she said. 'He might come across as caring and concerned, but if it came to a shootout between me and him, I bet he'd have no hesitation in pulling the trigger.'

Sally sighed. 'Why are all the hot ones such gits?'

Cynthia shrugged. 'Do you think he's hot?'

'He's blimmin' gorgeous. All the women in work think he is.'

Cynthia did think he was hot. She wasn't going to admit it, though – he was a colleague and a rival. And she was also pregnant.

Why lust after something you can't have? Not that she wanted him…

'It's a shame I'm a happily married woman,' Sally said. 'If I weren't, the things I could do with that man.'

'Sally!' Cynthia pretended to be outraged.

'Bet you would too, if you are honest.'

'I would not!'

'Go on, admit it; if you weren't feeling so poorly, you could think of a few things.'

'I'm pregnant.'

'So? It's not as though there's anyone else on the scene.' She hesitated. 'Is there?'

Cynthia's reply was soft. 'No.' That was the closest Sally had come to asking her about the baby's father.

'Well then. He's clearly into you,' her PA pointed out.

'I can't believe we're having this conversation. I'm your manager.'

'You're also a woman and he's a man, and we've known each other for how long? I think I've earned the right to be honest with you. He likes you. And I think you like him.'

'He probably likes a whole lot of people and I hardly know the guy. Besides, I'll say it again – I'm pregnant.'

'That doesn't mean you have to be a nun and dedicate the rest of your life to motherhood. You can be a wife at the same time, you know.'

'I'm not planning on getting married any time soon, and certainly not to Max Oakland. Have you been sniffing the Tippex again?'

Sally giggled. 'I don't use Tippex. But I am pleased you seem to be a bit better. How are you feeling? Can I get you anything?'

'I'm good thanks, and yes, I am feeling a bit more like myself. The antibiotics must be starting to work.'

'You still look as though you could do with a rest, so I'll be off. I don't expect you in tomorrow either.'

'Sally, about the baby's father... I'll be raising this child on my own. It's not going to be easy, and I'm, well, feeling a bit apprehensive.'

'I'm not surprised. Was it planned?'

'No.'

'Even more reason for you to feel nervous. You'll cope, though; you always do. But a word of advice – it's difficult enough to raise a child when there are two parents on the scene, and twice as hard when there is only one, especially when that parent has to go to work. Don't push yourself too hard. There are more important things in life than Ricky Webber's job. And think on this – it doesn't seem to have made him happy.'

'What I was going to say was, can you do me a favour and find out how to go about hiring a nanny? I know it's not in your job description, but could you start the ball rolling?'

'Oh. Sorry.' Sally worried at her bottom lip with her teeth. 'Yes, I can do that. I'll have something ready for you tomorrow and email it to you.'

'Thanks, and I'm very grateful you came.'

'You're welcome.' She grimaced. 'I didn't mean to say anything out of turn.'

'You didn't. But I do want Ricky's job and I don't intend to let being pregnant stop me.'

When her PA left though, it wasn't Ricky's job that was at the forefront of her mind – it was Max. What had Sally been on about? Max most certainly didn't like her, not in *that* way.

But even as she pushed the ridiculous thought out of her mind, a little part of her was wishing it was true.

Chapter 13

Goodness me, she thought two weeks later, having finally found the time to sift through the details Sally had sent her. There were so many variations on the degree and type of childcare on offer, and she wasn't totally sure that what she needed, what she wanted, and what she preferred, were going to gel into a single Mary Poppins package. There was also the issue of the salaries nannies can command.

Sally had been her usual thorough self, and had sent her some samples of adverts she could place herself, details of agencies she could use, day nurseries, and au pairs. So Cynthia was sitting on the living room floor, her back propped against a pile of pillows, with music playing softly in the background. Apparently the baby could hear by now, and music was soothing. She also had some snacks to nibble on in easy reach and a glass of milk. She would have preferred wine, but heigh-ho.

She hadn't considered the details, but it was about time she did. From what she had read online, she knew good nursery places were booked up months in advance, and she scanned one of the leaflets, frowning as she read the opening times. With a sigh, she put it to one side before picking up another.

That was just as bad. How was she supposed to get into work for six a.m., six-thirty at the latest, when most nurseries didn't open until eight o'clock? And assuming she could find one which did open early enough, hauling a baby half-way across the city before most people had eaten their breakfasts didn't appeal to her either. Then there was the inflexibility of a nursery, because from what she could see, they were quite rigid in their times. She couldn't guarantee to collect the baby at seven pm, no matter how much they insisted she should.

Plus, she noticed as she read one brochure after another, very few of them took babies under six months old. Great.

She put the last one down with a deep sigh. This lot was destined for the rubbish bin, because there was no way a nursery setting would work for her. She'd have to look into the nanny option again, which was what she'd originally intended to do before she saw how much she'd have to pay for one.

Her phone rang and she was glad for the interruption.

'Hi, Mum.'

'Just thought I'd give you a call to see how my little girl is.'

'Not so little. I'm turning into a whale.'

'Not you, I meant the baby. You did say you were having a girl, didn't you?'

'I hope so. That's what my gut instinct is telling me. I haven't been officially informed yet, though.'

'Oh, OK, so you don't know then.' Her mum sounded disappointed.

'I honestly do think it's a girl,' Cynthia insisted. 'And I'm very well, thank you,' she added archly.

'I wish I could see you. Are you sure you're eating right? And how are you sleeping? I remember when I was having you, I kept waking up every hour on the hour to go to the loo.'

Cynthia chuckled. 'I'm not at that stage quite yet.'

'It's horrid having you live so far away. How are you going to manage when the baby comes? They're a great deal of hard work, you know.'

Cynthia was wondering that herself – not the hard work part, because she'd never been shy at rolling her sleeves up – but the managing bit. Very briefly she considered suggesting her mum came to live with her, then she immediately dismissed the idea. Mum was nearly seventy – she'd done the motherhood bit, and while being a grandma might be enjoyable and fun, it would be vastly different to looking after the baby full time, especially since Cynthia often left for work at six and didn't get back home until eight in the evening or later.

After they'd said their goodbyes, Cynthia realised the decision regarding childcare had been made for her – she definitely needed a live-in nanny. It would greatly cut down on costs if she could throw bed and board into the equation, and thankfully she didn't work Saturday or Sunday, so the Mary Poppins person could have most of the weekend off. She seriously didn't like the thought of having someone else in her apartment, but what other choice did she have?

Her life was going to change completely, she realised. Gone was the idea that the baby would simply slot in. Having a stranger living in her home wasn't slotting in. It was a complete upheaval. So much for her previous naivety in thinking she'd be able to carry on much as she had before.

She eased her legs a little, cramp making its presence felt. Great, something else to add to the pregnancy related discomforts she'd experienced thus far. Swollen feet was the one which was getting to her the most at the moment, because she'd had serious problems putting her shoes on this morning. It had felt like she had been walking on broken glass all day, and as much as she hated to admit it, she'd have to invest in some flatter shoes.

She hadn't expected the heartburn either, and she rubbed the centre of her chest to ease the burn.

Sally, bless her, had bought her a pregnancy and childbirth book, and Cynthia heaved herself off the sofa to fetch it. Maybe it would have a suggestion or two in there as to what she could take for indigestion.

Two hours later, she was engrossed in it. At five months, or eighteen weeks pregnant, she was already nearly halfway through, and her baby was the size of an artichoke. She had to look it up on the internet, not being too familiar with that particular vegetable. She was fascinated to read her baby weighed about seven ounces and was roughly five inches long.

It was growing fast, the book informed her, and her uterus was expanding quickly to accommodate it. You can say that again, she thought. The new suits she'd bought were already straining at the seams, and it was getting more and more difficult to conceal her growing bump. The men she worked with were, for the most part, oblivious, but some of the women were beginning to give her speculative glances. It wouldn't be long before the rumour mill began grinding away, if it hadn't started doing so already.

It would soon be time to tell the Pitbull her news, and Cynthia wasn't looking forward to it one little bit. Just the thought of it made her insides churn. Great, now she had gas to add to the heartburn...

Her eyes widened and she stilled. The music was silenced; her living room disappeared, and the book in her hands was forgotten. The only thing she was aware of was the little flutterings inside, as she realised it wasn't indigestion she was feeling. And even though she'd seen her baby on a monitor, this was the first real indication there was another person inside her.

'Hello, little one,' she whispered softly, wonder and awe in her voice and her heart.

Her baby was alive and had just made her presence felt, and nothing in the world had ever made her feel so humble or so full of love.

Chapter 14

Cynthia grabbed her bag from where she'd stashed it under her desk, and heaved it onto her shoulder. It weighed a tonne and she made a mental note to clear it out when she had five minutes; which would be some time in the next century the way things were going. She could take the darned pregnancy book out of it, for a start, but she liked having it close so she could dip into it when the fancy took her. There was something comforting about having a physical book in her hands, and not a virtual one on her phone.

Lordy, look at the time. She'd be late if she didn't get a move on.

Barrelling out of her office door, she almost bumped into Max. He was distracted and there was a crease between his brows.

'We've got a problem,' he said, after catching hold of her by the elbows to steady her. 'Are you OK?'

'I'm fine. What problem?'

'Field Hotels are—' He spotted her bag on her shoulder and her jacket over her arm. 'Is this a bad time?'

'Yes, it is,' Sally replied, at the same time Cynthia said, 'No, what's up?'

Cynthia glared at her PA. Sally smiled sweetly back at her.

'She's off to her twenty-week scan,' Sally told him. 'And she's late.'

'Then I mustn't keep you,' Max said.

Cynthia was torn. In the short amount of time she'd been working with him, she'd come to appreciate that Max wasn't the type to say there was a problem if there was something he could do about it. His usual modus operandi was to inform her after the event, when he'd arrived at and had implemented a solution. Not that there'd been many problems to date, and none of them had been greater than little niggles. This must be something serious for him to want to share it with her at this stage, and her toes began to curl. There were several million pounds riding on the take-over, and they couldn't afford for anything to go wrong.

Max said, 'Go. It'll keep. I'll fill you in when you get back.'

Still she hesitated.

'Seriously, it can wait. Your baby can't.'

'Shhh!' She flapped a hand at him and glanced around nervously, although there was no one else in the office except the three of them. These walls had ears, and she often speculated how Ricky knew stuff he had no business knowing. Not for the first time she considered the office might be bugged.

Max pushed her gently towards the door, and Sally made a shooing gesture.

He was right, a couple of hours would make little difference and she'd never get the opportunity to see her baby at twenty weeks gestation again. So she went.

The antenatal clinic was a little more familiar this time, and although she felt the lack of a companion (every other mum-to-be had someone with them), she didn't feel as out-of-place as she had on the previous occasion. And she was going to meet her midwife, which she was thoroughly looking forward to. The woman's name was Jess, and she had been on holiday for her last visit, and Cynthia was anxious to meet the woman who was going to help her baby come into the world. The birth was the part of the pregnancy process Cynthia was studiously avoiding reading about. The idea terrified her, and she preferred not to think about it until nearer the time.

'Hmm.' Her midwife frowned at the blood pressure monitor. She was a lady of around Cynthia's own age, and she had an air of calm confidence about her. Cynthia had warmed to her immediately.

'Your blood pressure is slightly elevated,' the midwife observed. 'We need to keep an eye on that.'

She asked her a series of questions involving her sleeping habits, her diet, and other things, until they eventually arrived at what Jess said was the "birth plan".

Cynthia didn't have one. For someone who was meticulous in planning and pernickety about the details, she hadn't planned anything. The nearest she'd come to planning for the event was to hope it didn't hurt as much as everyone said it would and that it would be over quickly. She was perfectly happy for the moment with her baby safely tucked into her tummy, and she didn't want to think too deeply about the problem of getting it out.

'I expect you've gone through all the different options available to you, and have some preferences of what you might like, and what you don't want,' Jess was saying, 'but my advice is, we can certainly work on your birth plan but don't feel too bad if we don't adhere to it.'

Cynthia quite liked the idea of a plan, now she was aware she was able to make one. Plans meant control. She liked being in control, and so far, as far as her pregnancy was concerned, she'd felt anything but.

They discussed a few options (giving birth at home? no thanks!), the use of water (she didn't like swimming at the best of times), and the availability of pain relief. By the end of it she'd settled on a hospital birth with an epidural. The thought of being able to deliver her baby and not having to go through agony in the process made her feel quite euphoric.

She could do this – it was all under control.

Until, that is, Jess informed her she could possibly leave hospital in as little as six hours after giving birth.

'But I thought I'd be in for a good few days, maybe even a week,' she protested.

'Let's hope you aren't, because that means something hasn't gone to plan.'

'But you can't simply hand me a baby and expect me to get on with it.'

'It's your baby,' Jess pointed out. 'You'll be more comfortable in your own home, and you won't be abandoned – there will be so many people popping in and out, you're going to wish they'd all go away.'

The only people who might pop in was her mum, if she could pluck up the courage to travel to the city, and Sally, who'd bring her gossip from work along with the obligatory card and bunch of flowers. Abruptly, Cynthia felt very much alone, and slightly overwhelmed.

Pulling herself together, she decided the nanny (whom she had yet to sort out) would need to be ensconced in the apartment at least a week before her due date, so as to be there for when Cynthia was discharged from hospital.

Feeling better about things, Cynthia trotted off to have her scan. This was the part she had been looking forward to the most today.

After a tense wait while the sonographer checked the baby and took some measurements, she turned the screen around so Cynthia could get a proper look.

Oh, my word… There it was, her baby, and once again she was filled with wonder.

'Baby is sucking it's thumb,' the sonographer said, pointing it out on the monitor, and Cynthia's heart melted.

'Can you tell whether it's a boy or a girl?' she asked.

The woman smiled. 'Sorry, the angle isn't quite right.'

Darn it, Cynthia had been sure she'd have her suspicions confirmed today. Never mind, she was still convinced it was a girl. A little dark-haired daughter with a nose like hers and freckles scattered across it.

The image of the little girl sitting in a bath full of bubbles flashed through her mind, and as she made her way back to work, the memory of seeing her baby safe in her womb stayed with her.

While she waited for a taxi, she phoned her mum, wanting to share the good news about the scan. She wouldn't mention her raised blood pressure, for the same reason she hadn't told her mother about her UTI. Her mum would only worry, and she didn't want her to fret, especially since she lived so far away and popping in to check on her daughter wasn't an option.

To her disappointment, there was no answer on the landline. Her mum was always busy and she rarely remembered to take her mobile phone when she went out. Cynthia would try again later this evening.

She did want to share her news with someone though, and, weirdly, the only other person she had an urge to tell was Max.

Shaking her head at her silliness, she made her way back to work and whatever problem Max had found.

Maybe she'd tell him later…

But there was one person she definitely needed to speak to about her pregnancy, and she wasn't looking forward to it one little bit. That person was the Pitbull.

Good luck with that, she thought to herself. She was going to need it!

Chapter 15

It was time – she had to tell Ricky she was pregnant before someone else did it for her. Sally she trusted implicitly, and she kind of trusted Max too, in a way, because he'd not told anyone as far as she knew.

Clutching the MAT B1 form she'd been given at the hospital, which she apparently needed to give to HR so they could start the ball rolling on her maternity leave, she hurried towards Ricky's penthouse office and asked his PA if she could have a quick word.

'I'll see if he's available,' his PA said, then stared pointedly at her stomach.

Cynthia smiled her thanks and pulled her suit jacket around herself in a vain attempt to hide her bump.

Hang on a minute – why should she be ashamed of being pregnant? It wasn't something that should be hidden. Bringing a new human into the world was something that should be revered. It was Ricky who should be ashamed for making her feel this way. And if his mother hadn't been pregnant once, then he wouldn't be here, so he should be celebrating motherhood and not vilifying it.

'Cynthia, what have you got for me?' he asked, as she sidled through the door and stood before him like a naughty pupil in front of the head teacher.

Not a lot, she thought, wondering what the problem was that Max wanted to speak to her about. 'I need to speak to you about something personal.'

'Go on.' He was scrutinising her over the top of his reading glasses.

There was no easy way to say it, and Ricky preferred people to be direct, so she said, 'I'm pregnant.'

'I see.' His expression wasn't giving anything away, but she noticed the hand holding his pen had gone white. His gaze dropped to her stomach. 'How far along?'

'Twenty weeks, that's five—'

'I know how many months that is, but why have you only now decided to tell me? Who else knows?'

'Sally, my PA. I didn't tell her; she guessed.' It wasn't a total lie, and neither was her failure to mention Max.

Ricky was continuing to stare at her stomach. 'I'm not surprised she guessed, and if she has, you can bet others have too. I'll announce it tomorrow. In the meantime, you might want to consider handing everything over to Max. I can't risk any glitches or hold-ups on the Field Mouse Project.'

'I don't need to hand anything over. I'm perfectly capable of carrying on.'

'Where were you this morning? I checked your diary – you were booked out from ten-thirty until twelve. It didn't give a reason.'

Damn. Employee's electronic diaries were visible to certain people within the company, but she'd never thought that Ricky would be bothered to trawl through hers to see who she was meeting with.

'Antenatal appointment.'

His smile was false. 'That's what I mean.'

'It was two hours.'

'Two hours which should have been spent here. I don't know if you're aware, but the project had a few issues this morning.'

'I'm aware.' She was tempted to cross her fingers to ward off the lie. Once again, it wasn't a total falsehood; she had been notified there was a problem, she just didn't know the nature of it, that's all.

'What are you going to do about it?' he wanted to know.

'Speak to Max in the first instance,' she replied confidently.

'Don't bother. He can take it from here. Let him have all your files and notes, and the dates of any meetings.' He turned his attention to the papers on his desk.

Cynthia was dismissed.

As she turned to leave, anger roiling through her, she heard the Pitbull say, 'Congratulations. Don't forget to keep HR informed.'

She didn't bother replying.

Seething, she made her way to the lift, alternating between wanting to cry and wanting to shove Ricky's head in the shredder. This was the start of her being side-lined. And to top it all off, she'd not only been instructed to hand Max the reins, but she had to spend the afternoon interviewing nannies.

Never before had she felt like throwing in the towel. She'd had some tough times with Ricky and in the past she'd felt like taking her expertise elsewhere. She never had though, because she knew the job inside out, she knew the company almost as well as Ricky himself did, and she also knew one day Ricky would retire.

Now, though, she couldn't help wondering if the sacrifices had been worth it. She'd worked her socks off for Ricky and his company, and for herself, too, if she was honest, because she'd wanted to climb the greasy pole. And this was the thanks she'd got. She was aware she'd not been on the ball these past few weeks, and she understood it was going to get worse for a few months until the baby was born, but after that she'd be back to normal.

Without thinking, she marched into Max's office, past Jeffrey's startled PA (who was now Max's PA, by default) and slapped her MAT B1 form down on his desk.

'I've got to hand everything over to you,' she announced.

He picked up the form and scanned it. Then he looked at her, confused. 'What is this?'

Cynthia snatched it back. 'Never mind. Ricky wants me off the project.'

'I take it you've told him about the…?' He nodded at her tummy.

'What do you think?' She was perilously close to tears, which infuriated her even more. God, she was sick of being so damned emotional. Bloody hormones! 'Not that you're bothered. This is what you've wanted all along.'

'To run the Field Mouse Project?' He sounded incredulous but Cynthia wasn't fooled.

'And I expect you're hoping to step into Ricky's shoes when he finally hangs up his briefcase.' She knew she was mixing up her metaphors, but she didn't care. 'Well, congratulations, you've probably got your wish.' Once she had a child, there was no way Ricky would let her run the company – she realised that now. It simply hadn't been feasible, doable or realistic.

Max was staring at her in confusion. 'You couldn't be further from the truth.'

'Then why are you here?' she demanded. He'd clearly been brought in to replace Jeff, and with Ricky giving him sole control over the biggest project she'd ever handled, the Pitbull was making his intentions very clear indeed.

'Because Ricky made me an offer I couldn't refuse,' Max said.

Cynthia almost believed him, but Max turned away, unable to look her in the eye, and she knew he was lying. She also knew exactly what the offer was, and it was then she realised it didn't matter a jot whether she was pregnant or not – Ricky's job would never have been hers.

Chapter 16

In one way, interviewing for a nanny didn't seem important anymore, but old habits were hard to break and her work ethic was still very much alive and kicking. Obviously she couldn't do them at the office, so once again she slipped out, warning Sally not to put anything in the diary; she didn't want to give Ricky any more ammunition.

Sally had lined up three for her. Cynthia had chosen them, but Sally, bless her, had contacted them all and set the interviews up. She'd also given her a list of questions (some of which Cynthia would never have thought of asking) and had prepared a score sheet for her to use if she wished.

It was all very professional and rather clinical, which was the way Cynthia usually approached the hiring of staff, but somehow the process didn't feel right in this situation. She hated to admit it, but she just might have to go with her gut feeling.

When the first one rang the bell dead on time, Cynthia felt unaccountably nervous as she went to answer the door. The three nannies she was seeing all came from the same prestigious agency, with a reputation for exceptionally high standards and excellent staff. Sally had informed her that nannies from this particular agency were extremely sought-after, and some of them had even secured positions with the British monarchy.

This was all well and good, but such nannies came with a high price tag and even higher expectations. Cynthia was under no illusion she was being interviewed as much as she was interviewing them. And she was worried she'd be found wanting.

'Hello, you must be Bea. Come on in. Did you find me OK?' Cynthia gestured for the girl to step inside and showed her into the living room. 'Take a seat. Have you come far?'

'Kensington,' Bea replied.

She was wearing a navy dress, belted in the middle, navy brogues, and a navy hat with a narrow brim and a cream band. A jacket was folded neatly over her arm and in her other hand she carried a navy handbag. Although she was only twenty-four, Bea looked older. It must be the no-nonsense air, the lack of make-up and the hair twisted into a bun at the nape of her neck, Cynthia decided.

The girl certainly looked the part, and her CV was impressive.

'Can I get you some tea? Coffee?'

'No thank you, Ms Smart.'

'OK, shall we get on? What made you decide to become a nanny?'

'I love children, that goes without saying, and as I'm not ready to have my own yet, looking after other people's is perfect. I get to travel too, which is wonderful.'

Travel? Hmm. 'I do travel with my job but I won't be taking the baby with me,' Cynthia said.

'No problem. I don't always expect to go skiing every year.' Bea gave a tinkling laugh. From the sound of it, that was exactly what this girl expected to do.

'When are you available? I need someone to start as soon as the baby is born.'

'I'll be free after Christmas. The child I am nanny to at present will be going to boarding school in January.'

'Ah. My baby is due at the end of November.'

'The timing may not work, if that's the case.'

No, Cynthia could see that. 'I'll be in touch,' she said. 'See what arrangements, if any, we can come to.'

She didn't intend to arrange anything with this girl, and the nanny was probably aware of it, too. The pair of them hadn't gelled at all and she couldn't imagine sharing her home with someone in a uniform. These nannies might be the best in their field but none of them was for her, she realised, after meeting with the other two.

She simply didn't feel comfortable having anyone else in her apartment.

An image of her and her baby, just the two of them, popped into her mind, and she was abruptly overcome with a fierce envy for all those women who were able to stay home and look after their children.

Did she want that for herself?

Cynthia no longer knew what she wanted and thinking about it was giving her a headache. It was only five o'clock; she should return to work but she honestly didn't want to. She was tired, disconsolate, and worried, so she took herself, her bump, and her blinding headache off to bed.

She lay there feeling her little baby move inside her, and hoped to God she would be able to cope.

Chapter 17

Cynthia felt the baby shift position and she smiled to herself. Her little one was quite active – or else she noticed it more now that she'd been reduced to doing more mundane tasks. She still carried a hefty load of responsibility on her shoulders, but Operations Director level it most certainly wasn't. Although she'd never admit it to anyone, she was secretly enjoying the respite, but she couldn't help worrying about the future, nevertheless. Her dreams of being CEO were over. It had taken her a while, she admitted, but she'd come to realise she had been incredibly naive to think the position would automatically go to her when Ricky retired. Max's arrival had shown her that.

And even if Max wasn't on the scene, it would take a considerable amount of hard work and determination to make Ricky forget this particular director had to disappear off for assorted scans and antenatal appointments, and would then be on maternity leave for at least a couple of weeks.

'A couple of weeks?' her mum had laughed, when Cynthia had mentioned it. 'Make it a couple of months. More, probably,' she'd insisted; and Sally had agreed with her mother, when Cynthia had told her about the conversation.

And that was only the start of it, she was warned.

Cynthia couldn't help feeling bitter because, as a rule, men didn't have those sorts of issues to deal with. Take Ricky for example – he had three kids by three different women, and not once, to her knowledge, had he ever been forced to leave the office early to pick a sick child up from school, or hadn't been able to come in on time because Ricky Junior had an orthodontist appointment, or a school play to be sat through. All he'd done had been to throw money at the kids and their mothers, and ignore everything else.

Cynthia couldn't do that; she didn't *want* to do that. What she wanted was to be a good mum, but she also wanted to keep working, too. Her job was important to her; it had been her raison d'être for twenty years. She'd handled take-over after take-over, and watched Ricky's company grow from strength to strength, and a great part of that was due to Cynthia herself.

He'd give her a decent pay-off to get rid of her, she knew that, but she didn't want to go. Even if she was feeling tired and achy, her belly button had popped out, she often felt breathless and, to her horror, a web of stretch marks had appeared across her stomach and the tops of her thighs – hauling something the size of a coconut around was hard work and tiring – she still wanted to keep her job.

Darn it, she missed being in the thick of things; so when Max appeared in the doorway one afternoon, she was pleased to see him.

'I thought I'd give you an update,' he said.

'That's nice of you.' She was being sarcastic, but either he didn't realise it or he chose to ignore it. Her money was on the latter.

'Shall we do it here or do you fancy taking stroll and grabbing a coffee on the way?' he suggested.

Cynthia raised her one eyebrow. The offer was unexpected, but not unwelcome. The sun was shining, and she suddenly wanted nothing more than to feel its warmth on her face and a gentle breeze in her hair.

'Are you OK to take a short walk?' he wanted to know.

'I'm pregnant, not ill,' she retorted.

'Glad to see you've not lost any of your spirit.'

'Why should I have? Because the Pitbull has put me out to pasture, do you mean?'

'Not at all. Actually, I'm not sure what I meant – I was just trying to make conversation.'

'I'd change the subject if I were you,' she warned, reaching for one of the gorgeous soft-knit cardigans she'd purchased in a variety of different colours because they were less restricting than a tailored jacket and, at the moment, comfort trumped corporate fashion. Besides, it shouldn't matter what a person wore as long as they looked smart. Three-inch heels or a tie didn't make an employee any better at their job, and she'd been so relieved to ditch the stilettos she'd practically danced into the office the first time she'd left her heels in the wardrobe.

'Would you like to go out to dinner with me?' Max asked, startling her, as they made their way outside.

'Pardon?'

'You suggested I change the subject.'

'A dinner invitation wasn't quite what I had in mind.'

'Will you?'

'Why?'

'Because I think Ricky is behaving like a prat.'

'I don't need your pity or your charity.'

'I'm not giving you either. I want to talk to you.'

'Can't you do that after you update me? After all, I thought that was the reason for dragging me out of my office?'

'I wasn't aware of any dragging going on. You came with me willingly enough. I don't need to drag women.'

She bet he didn't. With those looks and with his confidence, he most likely had ladies falling over him. Sally was certainly one of them, and she was happily married. Cynthia was noticing the sideways glances given to him by many of the females they passed as they strolled along the pavement. He certainly didn't lack admirers.

Thankfully, she wasn't one of them, although she could appreciate a handsome man when she saw one, and Max was undoubtedly attractive.

'Is Ricky grooming you for the chief ex job?' she asked abruptly as they turned towards the entrance to one of the area's pretty parks.

'No.' He didn't even flinch.

That was straight to the point, but she wasn't sure whether she believed him. She wasn't sure she cared, either. He was welcome to it. These past two weeks she'd not been in work before eight and she'd been home by six-thirty. It was making her re-evaluate the nursery thing. And that wasn't the only thing she was reconsidering – the length of her maternity leave was also on the agenda.

'You said Ricky had made you an offer you couldn't refuse? What is it?' she asked.

'I'm sorry but I'm not at liberty to say.'

'I see.' He'd just confirmed her suspicion he had been brought in for one reason only, and that was to step into Ricky's hand-made leather loafers.

'You probably don't,' he said.

'Oh, I think I do.' He was being patronising and it got her back up. 'But one thing is confusing me,' she said. 'Why you? You're an outsider. I know I'm not exactly family, but I'm a better prospect than you. I'm a better candidate to run the company than any of Ricky's kids.'

Ricky's kids were hardly kids. They were around her age. Two daughters and a son. The daughters lunched, shopped, looked beautiful, and played tennis, and had no interest in his business except to enjoy the money they gleaned from it. His son spent all his time in and out of rehab. No wonder Ricky didn't trust them to look after his precious company. Although, when he eventually did step aside, he'd still retain the deciding share and he'd still have a seat on the board, so whoever wore the CEO title would wear it in name only, would be nothing more than a figurehead, and Ricky would still continue to pull the strings behind the scenes.

'I don't want Ricky's company,' Max said. 'It's the last thing I want.'

'I don't believe you.'

He shrugged. 'Believe what you like, time will tell. Let's get that coffee I promised you.' He gestured to the kiosk.

When they both had a hot drink in their hands, he led her to a bench. There were a couple of toddlers running across the grass after a ball, and Cynthia found herself unable to drag her attention away from them.

One of them, a girl, had a pair of dungarees on and a pink band in her dark hair, and Cynthia imagined herself bringing her own daughter to the park and playing ball with her, then taking her for an ice cream and—

'I'm going to recommend Ricky walks away from the deal,' Max said.

'Excuse me?'

'Field Hotels, it's not right for him.'

'He's already done all the background work on this,' she objected. 'He must have done, or he wouldn't have handed it over to me. Us.' She knew how Ricky operated. He found a struggling company, bought it out, and either turned it around or sold it for parts. His plan for Field Hotels was to revamp it and run it as a going concern. He hadn't shared the details with her – and neither did he need to. Her remit was – *had been* – to acquire the company at a decent price.

'If he has, he's missed something,' Max said.

'Like what? Ricky never misses anything.'

'He has this time. They have twenty-three hotels, right?

'So?'

'On average that's two-thousand seven hundred rooms, yes?'

'And?' Why was he telling her what she'd discovered within the first five seconds of Ricky handing her the project?

Cynthia sipped her tea (she was still off coffee) and listened to Max as he explained the reasons why he thought Ricky should walk away from the deal as it stood. And the more he talked, the more she realised his reasons were sound, financially and morally, and her respect for him grew, even if she still mistrusted him and his motives.

'You might be right,' she conceded, grudgingly. 'Are you going to tell him, or do you want me to do it? I'll also need to know how much this has cost the company so far.'

'I'll do it, but I'll send you the budget figures and the findings to date. And I also want to tell him it's all down to you.'

Cynthia stared at him, her mouth open, her mind whirling. 'Why?' She barked out the word. 'He took me off the project, if you recall?'

'Because you've put your heart and soul into this company and I haven't. Look, Cynthia, you're damned good at your job. I know it, you know it, and Ricky knows it. It doesn't make one iota of difference to me if you get all the credit for this. But it will make a difference to you. And, as I said, he's behaving like a prat.'

'And as *I* said, I don't need your charity.' She got to her feet. 'Thanks for the tea, but I have to get back. I've got some important shredding to do.'

He laughed, a deep rumble. 'You'll be telling me you're doing the filing next.'

'It feels like it. I can do the stuff I'm currently working on in my sleep.'

'Which is why I want to tell Ricky this is all down to you.'

'No. Absolutely not.'

Max inclined his head. 'Can we at least present a united front and give him our recommendations together?'

'They are your recommendations, not mine.'

'You do realise you're not ruthless enough for this, don't you?'

'I can be ruthless when I need to be, but I refuse to take credit for someone else's work.'

'That's admirable.'

'I sense a "but".'

He held up his hands. 'It's none of my business. You have to do what you are comfortable living with.'

'I can live with this,' she assured him. 'I'm a big girl; I can take care of myself.'

He sent her a sideways glance and she simply knew he was thinking about the scare when he had to take her to the hospital. She'd needed caring for then, all right, even if she'd been reluctant to admit it at the time. But this was different, this was business, and she hadn't got to where she had without being able to fight her own battles.

But as Max held the door to the foyer open for her and she walked into the building where she'd spent nearly all of her adult life, she continued to question whether she really did want to fight anymore.

Chapter 18

'I can't believe I'm doing this,' Cynthia said as a waiter pulled out a chair for her and she slid onto it.

Max looked amused. 'Don't you go out to dinner much?'

'Very funny. Not.' She opened the menu and scanned it. 'What did you want to talk to me about?' she asked, her eyes on the starter options, her mind on him.

She'd not seen him in anything other than a suit before, and he was even more handsome in jeans, an open-necked white shirt with the sleeves rolled up, and a tiny hint of stubble on his chin.

Dinner was in an Italian restaurant with gingham tablecloths, old chianti bottles as candle holders, and the heavy aromatic aroma of herbs and garlic in the air. She was glad she hadn't dressed too formally. The loose dress flowed over her bump and the colour suited her, she hoped.

'You look beautiful,' he said to her as she removed her cardigan.

The evening air had been a little cooler outside, but once inside the restaurant she was starting to feel quite warm.

'Thank you.'

'It's true what they say about pregnant women blooming.'

'Did that mean I looked hideous before?' she joked.

'I didn't know you before.' He closed his menu. 'OK, I've got you here under false pretences. I don't want to talk to you, I mean, I do, but not about work or anything. I apologise if I led you to believe otherwise.'

'Why would you do something like that?'

'Because you wouldn't have agreed to have dinner with me, otherwise.'

She made a moue. 'True, but I still don't understand why you asked me, though.'

'Because I thought you could do with a friend right now.'

She narrowed her eyes. 'I have plenty of friends, thank you.' It wasn't true, but he didn't know that.

'How are things? With the baby, I mean.'

'Great. We're both doing well. Did you know, she weighs about a pound now and she can hear my voice. She can probably hear yours too, so you'd better be careful what you say.'

'Motherhood suits you.'

Cynthia looked at him, startled. 'Thanks. I think. But if you're referring to the fact I've put on weight, you can take it back.'

He chuckled, a deep rumble which sent shivers through her. 'I'm not. It's just when I first met you, you looked stressed and uptight.'

'I'm not surprised! I'd only discovered I was pregnant the day before.'

'It wasn't a happy surprise, I take it?'

She hesitated. 'No, not at the time. I'd given up thinking I'd ever be a mother. I'd assumed the marriage and baby thing had passed me by.' She laughed, but it was a slightly bitter sound. 'The marriage thing is still definitely not on the cards. Me and bump will do just fine on our own.'

He was studying her intently.

'What?' she asked.

'If that baby was mine, I'd never let you bring it up on your own.'

Cynthia blinked, taken aback. What was she supposed to say to that?

'I admire you,' he continued. 'It can't be easy being a single mother.'

'I wouldn't know,' she quipped. 'I haven't tried it yet.'

'I gather you intend to carry on working once it's born?'

'Do you have a problem with that?'

He held up his hands. 'No need to be so prickly – I was just making conversation and showing an interest.'

She let out a sigh. 'Sorry, it's just everyone seems to have an opinion. No one thinks I can go back to work and bring up a child – in the first few months anyway. They all seem to think I need to take a decent chunk of maternity leave.'

He made a face. 'It's your life, it's up to you what you do with it.'

'Thank you!' She took a sip of her drink. 'I hate to admit it though, but my mother might be right. I'm seriously beginning to wonder whether I can do either as well as I want to. It's been so much easier since Ricky has taken me off the Field Mouse Project, but the respite won't last forever. He's not going to continue to pay me the big bucks for doing little more than admin work. He's going to want his pound of flesh sooner or later.'

'In an ideal world, what would you like to happen?'

Cynthia leant back, her hands on her tummy. The baby was doing acrobatics in there, as if she too wanted a say in the matter. 'I honestly don't know. I thought I did. Not so long ago I'd have sold my soul to become the chief exec. Now, though…?'

The memory of the last time she'd visited her mum swam into her mind. The pretty cottage, the clean air, the peace, the space… the *time*. Time to spend with her daughter, watching her grow.

But what would she do for a job? She'd have to work, and a sleepy little village near the south coast would hardly provide the kind of salary she currently enjoyed.

Then again, did she want the kind of job she had now? She'd still be in the same boat of early mornings, late evenings, and not seeing her baby. She'd be no better off – worse, in fact, because at least she knew what she was doing at Webber's. Working somewhere new would mean having to prove herself all over again. There wouldn't be a slower pace of life for her, just a change of scenery which she'd be too busy to appreciate. And she'd still have the issue of another woman bringing up her baby.

The only redeeming factor would be that her mum would be close at hand.

'Penny for them?' he asked, cutting into her pondering.

'I was thinking about where my mum lives and how wonderful it would be to bring up a child there.'

'Where does she live?'

'A village called Little Milling, near Chichester. It's wonderfully rural and full of community spirit.'

'Sounds nice; what's stopping you?'

Over their main course, Cynthia explained all the reasons why it wouldn't be practical, ending with, 'My life is here, in London.'

'Your life can be wherever you want it to be. But you don't have to make a decision yet, do you?'

She shook her head. 'I'm fed up of thinking about it. Anyway, enough about me, tell me a bit about yourself.'

He raised his eyebrows. 'There's not much to tell. I've got a sister who lives on the Isle of Wight, my parents live in Tuscany, and I live in London for the moment, although I do have a place in the New Forest.'

'It must be nice having a second home,' she mused. 'Somewhere to escape to on weekends.'

'It's not a second home. My flat in London is the second one, but I don't own it, I just rent it for the duration.'

'The duration?'

'I… er… I won't be staying in the city.'

'In London? But your job is here.'

'I'm not sure if it's for me.'

Cynthia put her knife and fork down and pushed her plate away. 'I don't understand.'

'I'm not at liberty to explain. All I can tell you is that this corporate life isn't for me anymore. It used to be; I used to thrive on it – but not now…' He trailed off.

'But Ricky—'

'I told you, I'm not interested in taking over from Ricky when the time comes.'

'Why did you replace Jeff, if that's the case?'

'Ricky… well, let's say he can be persuasive.'

She wouldn't have called the Pitbull persuasive. Bullish, domineering, overbearing… but not persuasive. Ricky commanded; he didn't *persuade*.

'One day you're going to have to tell me all about it,' she said.

'I will,' he promised. 'One day.'

Finding she believed him, she intended to hold him to it. As what he'd said sank in, she realised that maybe she did stand a chance of the chief executive role after all, and her heart gave a lurch.

Her baby moved inside her in response, and she stroked her belly absentmindedly, wishing she knew what she wanted and what she should do for the best – for her and for her daughter.

Why, oh, why was life so complicated?

Chapter 19

Cynthia, finding it hard to let go of her dream of the top job, spent the next four weeks hedging her bets, putting the work in now so she might not have to do as much later. It had been a struggle to go back to arriving in the office before the birds had woken and leaving after most people had settled down to watch *Corrie* or *EastEnders*, but she'd done it. She'd defied Ricky's edict to leave everything to Max, and had thrown herself into salvaging the Field Mouse Project, with a vengeance. Just in case...

Max was right though, Ricky should walk away from it. Any take-over would cost too much, especially since she discovered the Pitbull intended to revamp all the hotels.

'He wants to do what?' she asked Max after he returned from a meeting with Ricky.

'Remodel them. Reduce the number of bedrooms, and at the same time increase the cost to the guest.'

'He's losing the plot. Why would he think that's a good idea?' It was bad enough the chain was running at a loss and the directors of Field Hotels had unrealistic expectations – why make things worse?

'Blame me. I have an eco-hotel in the New Forest. Ricky seems to think that is the way forward, combining staycations with the eco movement.'

Cynthia paused for a moment before saying, 'He does have a point, but I assume you don't think so.'

Max shrugged. 'Anyway, that's his vision, but the way things stand at the moment, it won't work. All the Field Hotels are in town centres, not the ideal locations for eco anything, not at present. Eco-hotels need to become more mainstream for it to be accepted.'

When you say "eco" what exactly are we talking about?'

'To be truly ecological, you'd have to eat what you grow – that can be translated into resourcing food locally. Only use the power you generate yourself – try telling a bunch of paying guests they'll have to go to dinner without a shower because there hasn't been enough sunlight today and you haven't installed a wind turbine because you couldn't get the necessary planning permission. You could also try explaining how a composter toilet works, although I wouldn't fancy your chances.'

'Can a compromise be made?'

Max pulled a face. 'Yes, but I don't think that's what he intends to do. He's going to pay lip service to the idea, while carrying on almost exactly as before, but with the addition of bamboo toilet paper.'

'Ouch! That's got to be scratchy.'

Max sent her a look and she bit her lip, trying not to laugh.

'It's a thing, it honestly is,' he protested. 'Don't knock it until you've tried it. Anyway,' he shook his head, 'not only that, but Ricky wants to do it on a shoestring.'

'That sounds like the Ricky we all know and love,' Cynthia said, picking up her bag. She and Max were due to go for their weekly lunch. It was getting to be a habit. Dinner was too late and she was always too tired, so they had settled on lunch once a week to catch up.

After they were seated in Luigi's and had ordered their food, Cynthia asked, 'Tell me more about this eco-hotel of yours. When you said you had a place in the New Forest, I assumed you meant a house or a cottage, not a hotel.'

She watched as his face lit up. 'The main part of the hotel is the farmhouse, a converted barn and a couple of cowsheds, and the stables have also been turned into guest rooms. Plus there are some yurts, a few treehouses, and some old railway carriages on the site.'

'That sounds like an eclectic mix.'

'I was aiming to appeal to a wider range of guests, other than the traditional stay in a guest room in the hotel type of clientele. I cater to those who love glamping – the yurts are very well appointed – and those who love glamping with a difference; and you can't get more different than sleeping thirty feet above the forest floor.'

'What about the railway carriages?'

'They would have simply rusted away, so I repurposed them; using locally sourced materials, of course, and all of it salvaged from something else.'

'Is this the reason he brought you on board – for your expertise?'

'One of the reasons. My expertise is valuable, but if he'd had told me about his plans earlier, I would have told him he's wasting his time.'

'What are you going to do?'

'See the project through. He's determined to carry on with it, despite my recommendation. I made a promise and I'm going to keep it.'

'A promise?'

'A contract, I mean.' He looked away, and Cynthia had the distinct impression he wasn't telling her the truth again. Disappointment chafed at her – she thought they were past all that.

'I'm confused,' she said. 'What does Ricky think he's going to achieve? I can't imagine how Field Hotels will gel with what you've described. In truth, I can't imagine an eco-hotel. Is the main part of your hotel vastly different from anything Field Hotels run?'

'Why don't you see for yourself?' Max offered.

'Seriously?' Cynthia thought he must be joking.

'Seriously. You'll be better informed as to how to move forward with his plans if he does go ahead and buy Field Hotels. Between us, we can at least try to make him stick to the principles of being environmentally friendly.'

'That must mean you're definitely planning on staying around?'

'No, I'm not.' He began to shred one of the bread rolls in the basket on the table, pulling the soft crust apart. 'After this, I'm thinking of opening another eco-hotel, if I can get the financial backing. That's going to take all my time and energy.'

'Why don't you ask Ricky to back it?' she quipped. 'Give him a taste of what you do.'

Max grimaced. He clearly was not enamoured of the idea, and she didn't blame him. Ricky would want to take over and run the whole show.

'Well, do you want to see my hotel?' he asked.

'I'd love to. Thank you.'

'It's a bank holiday weekend the week after next. How about coming to visit it then?'

Cynthia wrinkled her nose. 'I would, but I wanted to spend a couple of days with my mum. I haven't seen her for ages, and with this one growing at a rate of knots, it'll be here before I know it.'

'Never mind,' he said. 'It was just a thought. Maybe another time?'

'How about if I come to yours on the Sunday?' she suggested, thinking furiously. 'I can go to Mum's on Friday, spend Saturday with her, then stay until Monday at yours, or even as late as Tuesday morning. But I have to be back in London by ten-fifteen on the Tuesday because I've got an antenatal appointment in the morning. I'll officially be in the third trimester,' she announced proudly.

'That's fantastic. Congratulations. Will your mother be OK with your new plans? I mean, if she was expecting you to stay the whole weekend…?'

'I was only planning on staying two nights.'

'It's agreed, then. But there's little point in both of us driving all that way. I more or less pass Chichester, so what if I pick you up here, drive us down and drop you off, then I'll come back to Little Milling for you on Sunday morning? I can drive us back to London early on Tuesday morning. Heck, I'll even take you straight to your antenatal appointment.'

'As long as you don't mind?'

'Not in the slightest.'

'It's a long time since I've had a proper break. I'm looking forward to it,' she said, acutely conscious that the last time she'd had a few days away, she'd come back pregnant.

'So am I,' he said.

When he smiled at her, her tummy did a funny little fluttery thing, and she was quite taken aback to realise it wasn't the baby who was making her insides go all quivery – it was him.

Chapter 20

For a bank holiday weekend, the weather was glorious, and as she stuffed herself into the passenger seat of Max's car, Cynthia felt as though she was off on holiday. She was looking forward to seeing both Max's hotel and her mum, and a few days away would do her good.

They didn't speak much on the drive (with one stop halfway because Cynthia needed the toilet), but she was content to listen to the radio and watch the world go by. The baby seemed to be bopping in time to the music and Cynthia smiled at the increasingly strong movements in her tummy.

Now and again she'd catch Max looking at her with an indulgent smile on his face, and she gathered he was as excited to show her his hotel as she was to see it.

But first, her mum.

It was barely noon when the car pulled up alongside her mum's pretty cottage. The honeysuckle was in bloom around the door and the garden was filled with flowers dancing in the faint breeze and the lazy drone of bees in search of nectar. It looked idyllic.

Cynthia struggled out of the car, her progress ungainly in her haste to wave Max off before her mum caught sight of him.

Too late…

He emerged from the driver's side at the exact same moment her mum opened the front door. Cynthia might have guessed it would be impossible to remain unnoticed – the lane was too quiet for that, and her mum would have been listening out for the noise of an engine.

'Cynthia, my darling girl.' Her mum hurried down the path, her arms outstretched, but her eyes were on the driver of the car and were alight with curiosity.

'Who's this?' Maggie whispered in Cynthia's ear as she enveloped her in a hug. 'Never mind, I'll introduce myself.' And she disengaged quickly, stepping around Cynthia with a nimbleness which belied her years.

'I'm Maggie, Cynthia's mum; and you are…?'

'Max Oakland, I work with your daughter.'

Cynthia leapt in, just in case her mother was harbouring any ideas. 'He was coming this way, so we thought it a good plan to travel together.'

'How lovely to meet you,' her mum said, smiling broadly, her face wreathed in wrinkles as her eyes crinkled. 'You'll stay for lunch, won't you? It'll be ready in less than an hour. Please say you will, there's more than enough for three and I never get to meet any of Cynthia's friends. She's so far away, you know, and so busy.'

Not that far, Cynthia thought guiltily, and she didn't have any real friends for her mum to meet. Work colleagues weren't the same, and neither would they want to be dragged halfway across the county to meet her old mum. Her mother also hit the nail on the head with the busy comment; yet another thing for Cynthia to feel guilty about.

Max hesitated and she didn't blame him. Her mum could be a bit excitable at times, and the poor man hadn't been anticipating being waylaid by a pensioner. He looked at Cynthia and raised his eyebrows, pulling a face which she interpreted as the offer being fine by him.

Cynthia nodded, and added, 'Please stay. My mum is a great cook, and as she says, she never gets to meet any of my friends. Actually Mum, as I told you, Max is a work colleague. He's on the board of directors and has taken Jeff's place. Remember, I told you about Jeff?'

Maggie looked blank. 'It's hard remembering all these people when you've never met them, so it's very nice to meet you, Max. I'll definitely remember you!'

'Thank you, I'd love to stay for lunch.' He sent Cynthia an amused look, which she chose to ignore. 'I'll just fetch your overnight case from the car.'

Cynthia linked arms with her mum and walked her through the hall and into the kitchen.

'He seems nice,' Maggie said.

'Yes, I suppose he is.'

'He's not *the one*, is he?'

'Pardon?'

'The *father*?' her mum hissed.

Cynthia's mouth dropped open. 'No, he's not! Now, shh.'

'Good. He's far too nice to be playing around.'

'Mum!'

'We're through here,' her mother called as they heard footsteps in the hall. 'If you could pop her bag upstairs, then come into the garden? It's far too nice a day to be sat indoors. Cynthia's bedroom is the first door on the left.'

Cynthia rolled her eyes. She was perfectly capable of carrying her own bag thanks, but her mum seemed determined to embarrass her. It was like being a teenager all over again. Yeuch.

She watched him stroll across the lawn and wondered why he was grinning from ear to ear; she was about to ask him when her mum leapt to her feet.

'You must be thirsty after such a long drive. Will lemonade do? I could offer you some gin to go with, but as you're driving… unless, of course, you'd like to stay the night?'

'Mum! You've only got two bedrooms,' Cynthia objected. Her mother was becoming unruly – it must be the novelty of Cynthia bringing someone "home".

Maggie gave an artful smile. 'I'm sure we'd muddle through.'

'He'll have lemonade,' she said through gritted teeth. Dear God, this was going to be a long couple of days.

Max was still grinning, and she made a face at him. He leaned closer and said, 'I like the pink wallpaper. Ballerinas are so you.'

'Shut up! My room hasn't been decorated since I was about twelve. And if this is going to be the tone for the rest of the afternoon, you can jolly well leave now.'

'Oh, no, I'm having far too much fun.'

'I'm glad one of us is,' she muttered.

Things settled down a bit after the lemonade was served, because Maggie kept having to pop into the kitchen to check on progress and she had less opportunity for mischief. Every so often a tantalising aroma of herbs and garlic wafted in their direction, competing with the perfume from the hundreds of flowers in the garden, and the heady scent of recently mown grass from one of the neighbours.

During one of Maggie's kitchen-dashes, Max leant back in the ornate metal chair and stretched out his legs, crossing them at the ankle. 'It's so peaceful here, and so pretty. Your mum must put a great deal of work into this garden.'

'She does. What with gardening, her WI work, visiting the old dears in the nursing home, the church, and the rest of the stuff in the community, she's always busy.'

'I want to be like her when I get to her age.'

'An annoyingly embarrassing old lady?'

He sniggered. 'She's funny.'

'Not from where I'm sitting.'

'I could still stay the night. It would be cosy.'

'You wouldn't fit in my bed, it's only a single.'

His gaze abruptly became intense. 'I'm willing to give it a go.'

A delicious shiver travelled through her, and she looked away. 'You'd have to sleep on the couch.' What was going on? Was he flirting with her or teasing her?

'In that case, I won't bother.'

'Good.'

'Lunch is ready,' Maggie called and Cynthia was grateful for the distraction. Flirty, teasing Max was hard to deal with. She honestly didn't know how to react, and the fact she was enjoying this side of him was also discomforting. She was reacting to him like a woman, and she shouldn't be doing that, not when he was a colleague and she was soon to be a mother. It was totally inappropriate. There was a part of her however (a considerably large part) which was enjoying the attention, revelling in it if she was honest, and she realised she was falling under his spell.

'I love your garden, Maggie,' Max said as they tucked into a hearty lunch of chicken casserole, new potatoes and fresh green beans from the allotment up the lane. 'The whole village seems charming. A perfect place to raise a family.'

He didn't look in her direction, but Cynthia knew the comment was aimed at her, and the situation was made worse when her mum enthusiastically agreed.

'Cynthia had a fantastic time living here when she was a child. Always up one tree or another,' her mother gushed.

Max bit his lip, and Cynthia had an urge to elbow her mum in the ribs to shut her up.

'A proper little tomboy she was,' Maggie carried on. 'Playing in the mud, collecting worms, making dams in the stream… I'd try and get her to wear pretty dresses and frilly socks, and play with her dolls, but it was no use. She loved being outside and was never happier than when she was covered in dirt.'

'I can't picture it,' Max said. 'She's so prim and proper now. It just goes to show looks can be deceptive.'

Cynthia shook her head and wrinkled her nose at him, then almost slid under the table with embarrassment when her mother said, 'I've got some photos in the dresser – I'll bring them out after lunch.'

'Don't you dare,' Cynthia warned. 'Max doesn't need to see photos of me in pigtails and dungarees.'

He was openly laughing, a sound which made her heart sing. 'I think I do.'

'Mum, you're not to show him. If you do, I'll leave,' she threatened.

#'How are you going to do that? I drove, remember?' he pointed out.

'I'll think of something,' she muttered. 'I'll walk if I have to.'

Max barked out a laugh. 'Was she this stubborn as a child?' he asked Maggie.

'Oh, yes, and the tantrums she used to throw were impressive.'

'Will the pair of you give it a rest? I'm beginning to regret coming here if this is how you behave,' she said to her mum, then she turned to Max. 'And I'm never bringing you here again.'

'Pity – I think your mum is ace.'

'And I think you are ace, too,' her mum declared, reaching across the table to pat his hand.

'When you two have finished…'

'Jealous?' Max asked, smirking.

'Never.'

'She is, I can tell,' her mum said.

Cynthia had never felt more relieved when Max eventually got to his feet, stretching his arms above his head and announced it was time he made a move.

Lunch had been a tricky affair, and she'd walked a tightrope of mortification and delight that Max and her mum had got on so well. The mortification had the upper hand, though, as she wondered how she'd be able to work alongside him after this.

Oh, wait, she wasn't supposed to be working with him at all, was she? Ricky had taken her off the project – so that was all right, then.

Except, it wasn't, because she was still working on it, and Max had gone from being a threat to being a friend. But the main problem was she was beginning to think of him in a decidedly not-friend way. More of a sexy available man way.

And that simply wouldn't do, especially since he was probably just being friendly. He most likely treated all women the way he treated her. He was a nice guy, and flirting must come with the territory of being so damned good-looking. She bet he didn't realise he was doing it.

'Max is nice,' her mother declared, after she'd enthusiastically waved him off with the tea towel she'd been holding. Cynthia had been more reserved, giving him a little wave then going back inside.

She was rather flustered to realise she was looking forward to seeing him again on Sunday rather more than she should be, under the circumstances. 'He is,' she replied, absently.

'What does he do? You did tell me, but I wasn't listening. I was too busy looking at his eyes. Have you noticed them? They're stunning.'

Cynthia sighed. 'He's taken Jeff's place on the board of directors. But I don't think he's staying with the company.'

Her mum's face fell. 'Why ever not?'

'He owns an eco-hotel in the New Forest, and I think he's going to concentrate on that.'

'That's a real shame, because he likes you. Are you sure you're just colleagues? You can tell me, you know; I'm your mother.'

'We work together – that's it.'

'I think he'd like it to be more. I saw the way he was looking at you.'

'You're mistaken.'

'I don't think so.' Maggie patted her on the arm. 'Don't let an opportunity for love pass you by – you never know when the next one will come along.'

'Mum…' Cynthia rolled her eyes. 'Even if you are right about the way he looks at me, and I'm not saying for one minute you are, you can't go throwing the L word around. I'm about to become a mother.'

'So?'

'I'm carrying another man's child.'

'So?' Maggie repeated.

'Who'd want to take that on?'

'From the look of him, I'd say your Max would.'

'He's not my Max.'

'He'd like to be, I'm certain of it.'

Cynthia wasn't certain. Far from it. He was just being nice, that was all. But her conviction didn't stop her from wishing her mum was right.

Oh, lordy, she was falling for Max Oakland, and there wasn't a darned thing she could do about it.

Chapter 21

Pagham had been her mum's suggestion and Cynthia looked forward to visiting the seaside of her childhood. She'd spent many a happy hour digging around in the sand and charging into the sea. First though, they had to get there, and after ten minutes in the car with her mum behind the wheel, Cynthia was beginning to regret it. She couldn't recall her mum being this cautious, or so nervous when driving. Maggie was incredibly slow, and for the first time it hit home her mum was nearly seventy. She was getting old, and Cynthia's heart constricted. How much longer would she be able to drive? No wonder her mum never visited her in London. She wouldn't have been able to cope with all the traffic, let alone the unfamiliar roads.

'When was the last time you went to Pagham?' Cynthia asked.

'Let me see; it's got to be at least ten years, maybe longer,' her mum said, which might explain her caution. Those once familiar roads were distant memories, but Cynthia couldn't shake off her worry. It didn't help that her mum flinched and swerved when a motorbike zoomed past, or the anxious glances into the rear view mirror when another vehicle drove too close.

Cynthia was pleased they'd come however, as she slipped off her sandals and walked barefoot across the wide expanse of sand. Maggie had carefully parked the car, changed out of her driving shoes (did people still do that?) and was now scuffing her way through the fine sand and complaining it was getting in her pumps.

'Take them off,' Cynthia suggested, 'and we can have a paddle.'

'A paddle?' The way her mum said it, "paddle" sounded like a dirty word.

'Yes, paddle. Come one, you'd better get some practice in, because I bet Bump will head straight for the sea as soon as she's old enough to toddle.'

'Oh, all right. I warn you, it'll be freezing.'

'I don't care, it'll be fun.'

Her mum looked dubious, but she took her shoes off, and those strange pop-sock things she was wearing instead of tights or proper socks, and rolled her trousers up to her knees. Cynthia hitched the skirt of her maternity dress up and tucked the hem into her knickers, so the rest of it billowed around her thighs. She must look a fright, but she didn't care.

'How are you, truthfully?' Maggie asked, linking her arm through Cynthia's as they headed for the edge of the sea; the tide was out so it was some distance away, glittering in the sunlight and looking rather inviting.

'I'm good.'

'Are you getting enough rest? I do worry about you, working those long hours.'

'They're not quite as long these days, not since Ricky took me off the project I was working on with Max.'

'That was kind of him.'

Cynthia snorted, a most unladylike noise. 'I don't think being kind was his intention.'

'Still, if it means you don't have to work so hard…'

'I suppose.'

'Are you eating well?'

Cynthia smiled fondly down at her. 'Yes, Mum.'

'Speaking to you on the phone isn't the same as seeing you with my own eyes. I must admit you look well. Pregnancy suits you.'

'That's just another way of saying I've put on weight,' Cynthia joked.

'You're still slim. Apart from this.' She patted the bump gently.

Cynthia stopped walking. 'She's bouncing around it there. Can you feel her.'

The wonderment on her mum's face brought tears to Cynthia's eyes and she brushed them away surreptitiously. The future might be uncertain, but there was one thing she was sure of, and that was she intended to spend more time with her mum.

If her mum would have her, she would like to stay with her for most of her maternity leave.

Sod going back to work in two weeks. She'd take at least six weeks, then re-evaluate the situation. People were right, she'd never get back those precious first weeks, and she owed it to herself and her baby to not rush back to work. She wouldn't spend too long at her mum's though, because having a tiny baby in the house would wear her out.

'I just hope I'll be around long enough to see the baby grow up,' Maggie said in a matter of fact voice, and this time Cynthia let her tears fall.

'Oh, Mum, don't say that. I'm sure you will; you're not that old.'

'I'm old enough. I'll be seventy-nine when it's ten, and eighty-seven when it's eighteen.' Maggie wiped her eyes with the back of her hand. In a brighter voice, she said, 'Anyway, do you know what you're having yet?'

Cynthia shook her head. 'They couldn't tell. I've not got another scan booked, but I suppose I could pay for one privately. I'm fairly sure it's a girl though.' A pretty girl with dark curling hair and freckles…

'Don't go setting your heart on a girl, because it might not be. Any thoughts on names?'

'I quite like Hannah.'

'Your grandma's name was Hannah.'

'I know.' The pair of them shared a smile.

'What if it's a boy?' her mum wanted to know.

'I haven't thought about it, but maybe… Evan?'

Maggie's smile was so wide it rivalled the beach. 'Your dad would have been thrilled.'

'I know. You don't talk about him much.'

'I don't need to. He's always in here.' Her mum put a hand to her heart. 'But if you want to, that's fine by me. He might be gone, but he certainly isn't forgotten, and naming your baby boy after him, means he never will be.'

They were silent for a while, each of them lost in their own thoughts. Then her mum spoke.

'I'm glad you knew him, and even more glad you have so many great memories of him. He was a wonderful man. It was such a shame he died before his time.'

Cynthia thought back to that awful day over thirty years ago when she realised her father was gone. She'd been eleven, and for a while her world had fallen apart. How different might her life had been if she hadn't lost him; she'd made a vow that night, while her mother had slept fitfully beside her, that she'd make him proud, that she'd make something of herself in her father's memory.

She wasn't sure she'd achieved what she'd set out to do, but she understood he'd be delighted at this new life she was carrying.

'I wish my baby could have what I had with Dad,' she said in a small voice. 'She – or he – won't know its father.'

'Oh, my darling girl, it doesn't matter. The baby will be loved and cherished regardless, and you never know, you may meet a man who will love and cherish you both, and will be a father to him or her, as well as a husband to you.'

'You never did.'

'I never found anyone to compare with your dad. I looked, but no one lived up to him and I didn't want to settle for second best.'

'Do you regret that?'

'Of course I do! Love makes the world go around, and I would have loved nothing better than to have found it again with someone else. But it wasn't to be. You, on the other hand, could find it with Max. Or are you heartbroken about the baby's father, because if you are, you don't act it.'

'I'm not heartbroken. I didn't love him, not even a little bit.'

'Then it's not too late for you. If you have a chance of happiness with Max, grab it. I bet any money he'll be a great dad. And another thing...' Her mum paused, the sad look replaced with mischief.

'What?'

'I bet he's good in bed, too!' Maggie giggled.

'Mum! You've done nothing but embarrass me since I got here. Do you intend to keep this up until I leave?'

'Definitely. Let's walk back and have a pot of tea and a slice of cake at the little café we passed, and I'll tell you all about the time you did a wee behind the vicar's chair. I expect you've forgotten, but I remember it like it was yesterday...'

Cynthia drank her tea and listened as her mother regaled her with stories from her childhood, some of which she remembered well, and some of which she'd totally forgotten, and throughout it all, she recalled the joy of growing up in a place where she could grub about in the garden, and play in the woods at the rear of the house. She remembered building dens in the ferns, dibbling about in the stream for pond skaters, and watching frogs' spawn turn into bullet-headed tadpoles. She could still taste the thrill of picking wild blackberries, and the shrieking excitement of the old rope swing which hung over a ten-foot drop and creaked alarmingly as it flew through the air.

The scent of growing things and fresh air had been intoxicating, and she'd been high on life and laughter, and she knew without a doubt she wanted the same for her own daughter.

As she listened to her mother's stories and played back her own memories, she understood she was trapped by her need to earn enough money to support herself. How she'd dearly love to live closer to her mother, but house prices in and around Chichester were just as expensive as London. Her chic apartment would buy her a two, possibly three bedroomed house here, but there wouldn't be anything to live on afterwards, and she found herself going around in circles in her mind as the endless argument of the necessity of having someone to look after her baby for her while she went out to work, vied with her need to be with her child as she was growing up, and spend more time with her elderly mother.

Fed-up of having this conversation with herself yet again, she let out a huge sigh.

'You don't have to go back to London,' her mum said, and Cynthia realised what her mother had been doing in telling her stories about her own childhood. 'You can move in with me. For a while at least, until you get on your feet.'

Cynthia's smile was small. 'I'm already on my feet, Mum. I have a good job and a nice apartment.' Which was true, although the thought of moving back home was tempting. Not tempting enough to make her forget Mum wouldn't be able to cope with a baby in the house, let alone in a couple of years' time, when said baby turned into an energetic toddler.

The only other option if she wanted to move out of London was to consider going further afield, but even then the equity from her apartment would only stretch so far after she'd bought her and her baby a place to live. She still had to find a job at some point.

'You don't need to decide now,' her mum was saying, unconsciously echoing Max. He'd told her the exact same thing. Her due date wasn't for another three months yet, and then there was the maternity leave she intended to take – although she would have to check out how long she was entitled to, and the terms and conditions. And the pay, too.

How much was that, anyway? She needed to find out before she made any plans or decisions.

There was one thing she was sure about though, and that was she no longer wanted to run Ricky's company. And she was fairly certain she didn't want the job she currently had, either.

Chapter 22

'You'll stay for lunch, won't you?' Maggie asked Max when he came to pick Cynthia up the following morning. It seemed to have become something of a mantra for her. 'I'm cooking roast beef.'

Is that why her mum had shoved such a large joint into the oven earlier? Cynthia had naively assumed it was because her mum liked to feed half of the village – she always took a Sunday lunch around to Mr Williams next door – but it appeared her sneaky mum was already plotting to persuade Max to stay a while.

'He can't, Mum, he's got places to be, people to see,' Cynthia said, feeling awful about lying but she wasn't up to sitting through another meal with the pair of them. Not so soon – give it a couple of weeks and she might have recovered from the previous ordeal.

'That's a shame – I didn't get to show you Cynthia's baby photos.'

'It was good to see you, Mum,' she butted in. 'I'll visit again soon, I promise.' She gave her mother a quick hug and ushered a bemused Max out of the door.

'Nice to see you again, Maggie. I can pop in another time to see those photos. I'm often passing, so it's easy to call in.'

'You wouldn't dare,' Cynthia hissed.

'Watch me,' Max said out of the corner of his mouth.

Maggie trotted behind them down the path and, as Cynthia opened the car door, her mother whispered in the loudest voice possible, 'Remember what I said about the way he looks at you,' then stepped back with a huge smirk on her face.

'What was all that about?' Max wanted to know was they drove off.

'Nothing. She was talking about next door's dog,' she improvised.

'Eh?'

'You had to be there.'

The journey was mostly motorway and not very inspiring, but once they'd left the dual carriageway they were soon travelling down narrow leafy lanes with woodland either side, interspersed with the occasional open field. Cynthia felt as though she was in a different world.

After driving through a particularly dense forested area, she said, 'This is what I imagined the New Forest to be.'

'Haven't you been here before?'

'Not that I can remember. With the sea so close, we tended to go there instead. That's where Mum and I went yesterday. We had a pleasant stroll along the beach.'

'I think your mum is great.'

'Believe me, the feeling is mutual. She was all over you like a rash.'

Max chuckled. 'I tend to have that effect on women of a certain age.' He was obviously joking, and Cynthia wondered if he knew just how devilishly handsome he was. Surely he couldn't have got to forty-five and not realised it?

'Here we are,' he announced, taking a sharp left through a set of open, rickety gates and easing the car down a narrow, tarmacked track which was only wide enough for one vehicle at a time.

'Oh, my word, it's divine,' she cried as the trees opened up to reveal several stone buildings laid out in an open-sided rectangle.

It was easy to tell which was the original farmhouse, and which had once been a barn and a cowshed from the shapes of them, but that was the only thing which gave away their origins.

'I was expecting something much more rustic,' she said, gazing around her. It looked more like a luxury hotel. 'Where are the solar panels and wind turbines?'

'We do have solar panels, you just can't see them from here. Most of our energy is provided by biofuel from agricultural waste from the farm over the way.' He waved an arm to his right. 'It's our main source of fuel, as well as providing us with dairy produce, fruit, and veg.'

'I'm beginning to see what you mean about Ricky's idea not being feasible. Weird, though, because it's unlike him not to do his homework. Do you think he's losing it?'

'I doubt it,' Max replied, lifting her overnight bag out of the boot. 'Let's get you settled in, then I want to show you around. Don't worry, you're not in one of the treehouses, or even a yurt. I've put you in the main house.'

'Where do you live?'

'See that cottage over there.' He pointed and she followed his finger to a small cottage partially hidden amongst the trees. 'That's me.'

'It's so cute.'

'I suppose it is. I never thought of it like that. It's convenient, that's all.'

'It reminds me of my mum's house. Have you got green fingers?'

He grimaced. 'Not so as you'd notice. I stick a plant in and hope for the best. I'm afraid my garden is rather more lawn than flowers, unless you count the ones growing wild all around it.'

The interior of the farmhouse was every bit as enchanting as the outside, with exposed stone, original fireplaces, beams and wood everywhere.

'This is some farmhouse!' she exclaimed.

'I've tried to keep it as is, where I can. This was once the sitting room, but it's now the reception area, but there is another room through there, grandly called the parlour, for guests to use, and a snug with a garden room attached. What was once the kitchen is now a utility room – as you can imagine, there can be a great deal of wet clothes and muddy boots, so guests can leave them in there to dry in time for their next adventure.'

He took a key off a hook and she followed him up the curving staircase, running her hand along the polished bannister. Plush carpet was under her feet, muffling her footsteps, and the walls were adorned with curious old paintings and artefacts. A cuckoo clock chimed once, making her jump.

'Don't worry, it doesn't come out to play at night,' Max said. 'Guests don't want that cheery sound waking them up every hour on the hour. This one is yours.'

He opened a door, and Cynthia stepped into a large room with an old fireplace, wooden floorboards covered by a massive rug, and a view of the forest.

'It's divine!' she exclaimed, sitting on the bed and bouncing slightly.

'Nothing in this room is new, and that applies to the hotel as a whole generally. Some things have to be, like the towels and the bed linen, but we've reused and recycled as much as possible. At one point I was such a regular at the local reclamation yard, I thought they might offer me a job. I'll leave you to freshen up, then how about meeting me in the parlour in half an hour for some lunch?'

Cynthia agreed enthusiastically; she was starving – as usual – and the promise of fresh, local ingredients already had her salivating.

After a quick wash and a brush of her hair, she unpacked, marvelling that everything seemed pretty normal. She wasn't quite sure what she'd been expecting, but the loo was the usual kind, the shower was high pressured and hot, and there were the usual accoutrements of hairdryer, kettle, and TV.

There was, however, not a teabag in sight. Instead, there was a selection of loose-leaf teas in little jars, and the teapot had a strainer built in. The milk came in the most delightful little bottles, stored in a tiny fridge, and there was a selection of biscuits wrapped in strange cloth. The treats were clearly homemade, and she helped herself to one even though she was about to have lunch shortly. It tasted as delicious as it looked.

'What's the stuff the biscuits were wrapped in?' she asked, as soon as she entered the parlour where Max was waiting for her. She stopped and gazed around the pretty room, which was filled with sunlight and old books. A log burner sat in the corner, wood piled alongside as well as a large wicker basket filled with dark green bricks.

Max noticed the direction of her gaze. 'We light the fire occasionally in the winter months,' he explained. 'We try not to burn too much, because it sort of defeats the object in trying to be more environmentally friendly, but all the wood are offcuts and the bricks are horse manure. Oh, and the wrapping for the biscuits is fabric coated with beeswax. It can be wiped over and reused again and again.'

Cynthia hardly heard him – she'd become stuck at the manure comment and was finding it difficult to move on from it. 'Manure? Really?'

'Yes, really. It smells of grass when it's burning, and the ash makes good fertiliser.'

'Gross.'

His laugh filled the room. 'Can you imagine Ricky doing that in his hotels?'

Cynthia couldn't imagine anyone, anywhere doing that. Ever. Yet, the evidence was in front of her eyes. She'd take Max's word for it regarding the aroma.

'Come on, let's go eat. Phillipe is the resident chef,' he began, leading the way through a door in the reception area which opened onto a large, bright dining room. 'He's responsible for designing the menu, which is influenced by what is in season and what is at its best right now. He's also a keen forager, so you can expect to find things like nettle soup on the menu.'

It wasn't on the menu today, however sautéed hedgehog mushrooms with spinach and sheep sorrel was (she assumed the mushrooms had nothing to do with real hedgehogs) so she had that to start and traditional roast lamb for her main course. Blackberry custard tart was her pudding of choice.

They chatted easily throughout the meal about all kinds of things and none of it was about work, to Cynthia's relief. It was as though Ricky and the company simply didn't exist on the same plane as Max and his hotel. His pride in it was obvious, but it was also clear he took nothing for granted, and his eagle eye was everywhere.

Every now and again his gaze came to rest on her face, and once or twice she was aware of him watching her, but when she looked his focus was on something else. But once, just once, their gazes locked and what she saw in his eyes made her pause.

And she began to wonder if her mum might be right.

Chapter 23

'Are you up to walking that lot off, or would you prefer to sit in the garden room, or on the terrace? You don't have to do anything if you don't want.' Max shifted in his seat, his normal easy confidence replaced by a faintly apprehensive expression.

'A walk would be nice. I don't think I can sit down much longer anyway, not with that huge lunch – which was absolutely delicious, by the way – and the baby competing for space.'

'Don't worry, we won't go too far. There are some pretty circular paths which aren't at all arduous, and if you get tired, just say.'

'I'm sure you'll take good care of me,' she said, levering herself to her feet.

'I most certainly will,' he replied.

There it was again, *that look*, the one which was filled with something more than friendship, but she wasn't quite sure what. It gave her goose bumps, in a nice way. A *very* nice way.

If she was forced, she'd have to say he looked as though he wanted to eat her up and wrap her in cotton wool, both at the same time. It was quite unsettling, as her fluttering insides was a testament to. She tried to blame her feelings on the baby moving, but she knew it wasn't. She was all aquiver and it was Max's fault. Or rather, not his, but her reaction to him. She'd not felt this way before, not with any man. This wasn't lust, or attraction (although she did feel both, and rather strongly). It was a much deeper emotion. Oh hell, she was more than falling for him – she'd *fallen*.

Damn and blast if she wasn't half in love with the guy.

It was all his fault; he was too darned nice. If he'd been a bastard, then those good looks of his might have excited her libido but that would have been it. But he'd touched her heart and her mind, and she had no idea what she was supposed to do about it.

To cover her confusion, she busied herself with slipping her cardigan back on and checking her phone hadn't fallen out of her pocket, and by the time she'd done that he was by her side and gesturing towards the door.

Cynthia felt as though she was waddling, not walking, as they started down a shady woodland path because she was so full, but gradually the meal settled and she sauntered beside him, the dappled light calming her nerves and the birdsong filling her ears.

Woodland, she discovered, had a smell all of its own, of green things, and of earth, and the air was particularly fresh and wholesome.

'Look, there – a squirrel.' Max took hold of her elbow and turned her slightly.

She squinted through the tree trunks, unable to see it at first, but then the little creature moved, spiralling jerkily up the trunk of a large oak until it disappeared into the canopy.

'Will we see any ponies?' she asked, trying to ignore the wonderful warmth of his hand on her bare skin, and the subsequent disappointment when he removed it. His touch had done strange things to her insides, and she could smell his aftershave too, an intoxicating blend of musk and citrus. The urge to lean in for a closer sniff was hard to ignore, so she moved away a step and craned her neck, pretending to look for the squirrel again.

'Probably not, the woods are a bit too dense for them here; they prefer the heath and pastureland, but you never know, if we're quiet we might spot a deer. Fallow are the most likely, although the only part you'll probably get to see of them is their black and white bottoms as they bound away. They're not keen on people, and I don't blame them.'

'Oh?'

'They've been hunted for over nine hundred years. It's illegal now, thankfully, but I get a feeling the adults whisper stories about us humans to their fawns to make them behave.'

Cynthia smiled and shook her head. 'You're silly.'

He might be, but her mum was right about something else, too – he would make a great dad. She could imagine him bringing her daughter into these woods and showing her their secrets, the hidden places full of toadstools and fairy glens, where hedgehogs roamed and dragonflies danced.

Hark at her!

She was going a bit daft herself. It must be the hormones scrambling her brain. She'd read mothers-to-be could get nesty in the days and weeks before the birth of their babies, but instead she was starting to look at men as potential father material.

Not men, a little voice in her head pointed out – *just the one. Max.*

They didn't see any deer and Cynthia honestly hadn't expected to, but she did see a treehouse. And it was simply enchanting.

Everything was constructed out of wood, even the circular window frames which looked remarkably like portholes or hobbit windows. A staircase wound its way around a trunk, leading to an outdoor decked area and the main (only?) door to the structure. It was far larger than she'd anticipated and wasn't constructed in the branches of a single tree as she would have imagined, but was built between the trunks of three massive trees.

'Fancy a pot of tea?' Max asked, and she blinked. Where was he going to get a pot of tea—? Oh.

'Isn't there anyone staying there?' she asked, tilting her head back as she examined it.

'Not until tomorrow. Would you like to see inside, or do you think the steps would be too hard to manage?'

'I'll be fine,' she said, but she loved the fact that he insisted on going behind her to make sure she didn't slip. What she wasn't so happy about was that her bottom was at his eye level and he could undoubtedly see every squidge and bulge as she trudged up the steps ahead of him.

Once she reached the top though, she forgot about her backside and her laboured breathing (those steps were high!) when all she could see was trees. She was surrounded by them, and the effect was magical and more than a little surreal.

She paused to admire the fantastic view before reluctantly turning towards the door Max was holding open and—

'Wow! I mean, seriously, wow,' she exclaimed.

'Nice, isn't it?'

'Nice doesn't cover it, nice isn't even close. When can I move in?'

'You might find it a bit cramped with a baby,' Max joked. 'There is a separate bedroom and a bathroom in the tree over there, but…'

'Don't care. I love it. How can you live in a mere house when you own something as wonderful as this?'

'Indoor plumbing? Heating? The house stays still?'

'Excuse me?'

'Treehouses can move a little when there's a strong wind. I prefer my sofa to stay still.'

'Is that all? You're a wimp?'

'I am?' There was a glint in his eye.

She nodded, grinning, enjoying the back and forth teasing. *Flirting* was the correct word for what they were doing, the little voice told her.

Without warning, he strode past her onto the decked area, and threw himself over the side.

Cynthia let out a scream and dashed after him, her heart pounding as she imagined him lying broken on the ground below, and she ran to the railing – to see him standing safely on a walkway below and laughing fit to burst.

'You scared the daylights out of me!' she cried, her hand on her chest. She felt certain her heart was about to leap out of it and her knees felt weak.

He stood there, grinning like a fool, and Cynthia swayed then slowly sank to the floor.

'Cynthia! Cynthia, are you all right? Shit! I'm sorry, hang on!'

She lay in a crumpled heap with her eyes firmly shut, hearing his harsh breathing as he hauled himself over the railing.

He was kneeling at her side and cradling her in his arms before she had a chance to move.

Cynthia held her breath. She'd intended to sit up and shout 'Gotcha!' as soon as his feet had hit the deck but it felt so good to be held by him, she let herself go limp, enjoying the moment.

'Cynthia? I'm sorry, so sorry. I didn't mean to scare you.' He sounded frantic, and she knew she couldn't keep up the pretence, so she opened her eyes and smiled wickedly up at him.

Oh, God, his face was inches from hers, his expression full of concern. But when the realisation slowly dawned that she'd got her own back, the worry changed to something else entirely.

With a rumbling groan, he scooped her to him. His lips found hers, crushing them, his mouth urgent and demanding. For a second she was too shocked to respond, then her arms came up and she gripped the back of his neck, drawing him deeper towards her.

His embrace tightened and he let out the faintest of moans, his tongue finding hers, teasing and tantalising, kissing her so thoroughly she thought she might faint for real. Her head swam and her pulse throbbed, tingling desire shooting through her, until the only thing she was aware of was his mouth and her heated response to his kiss.

Abruptly he pulled away.

Her lids had floated shut when his lips first touched hers, but they abruptly flew open. She stared at him in dismay. Her mouth throbbed, and she felt hot and filled with a strange languid excitement which was making her heart pound and her breath sound ragged in her ears.

His eyes blazed with a heat that burned in its intensity, and she thought he was about to devour her – then the hunger faded as he lowered her gently to the deck and rocked back on his heels.

He licked his lips and she resisted the urge to lick hers. She could still smell him and the taste of him lingered on her tongue. She lay there, too shocked at the desire she felt to move, wondering what he was going to say or do next. Desperately wanting him to kiss her again, she willed her pulse to slow and her body to stop fizzing.

'I should say I'm sorry,' he muttered. 'But I'm not.'

Neither was she, although she wasn't going to admit it.

And neither was she sorry when, with a soft curse, he gathered her to him again and kissed her until she was breathless once more.

Chapter 24

Max released her slowly, and Cynthia gradually came back to the world, regret coursing through her. Although, she wasn't 100 per cent certain what the regret was for – for him ending their embrace? Or for instigating it in the first place? Whatever the reason, it was going to make life awkward from now on. How was she supposed to continue a professional relationship with a guy who kissed like that? With a guy who made her feel more alive than she'd ever felt before. A guy who made her heart sing and her soul fly.

To be honest, how good a kisser he was shouldn't factor into it. Putting her feelings to one side, the fact that they'd kissed at all was the relevant issue, surely?

But oh my God, it had been good. She had just been kissed with more passion and thoroughness than she'd ever had the delight of experiencing, and she was still reeling from it. Her blood pressure had gone through the roof and her heart was still thudding alarmingly. It couldn't possibly be good for the baby, and it most definitely hadn't been good for their working relationship, but it had been the most wonderful kiss (kisses – there had been more than one, she reminded herself) she'd ever had. And she had no doubt if he wanted to kiss her again, she'd let him. And more.

Please let him kiss her again…

Instead, to her intense disappointment, he held her to him tenderly, her head against his chest, and she could hear her own frantic heartbeat echoed in the thud of his, and his breathing was as quick as her shallow gasps for air.

She could feel the tension thrumming in him, mirroring her own.

God, but she didn't want this to end. In fact, she wanted to—

The mood was broken when he gently released her and got to his feet.

She lay on the deck, staring up at him, feeling bereft and frustrated. It simply wasn't fair of him to practically seduce her, then leave her wanting more.

Or, come to think of it, maybe he was being sensible and she was acting like a cat in heat.

Cynthia blamed it on her pregnancy hormones.

Max held out a hand and helped her get to her feet, the muscles bulging in his forearm, and briefly she wished it was still wrapped around her, holding her close. He didn't say a word, but the hunger on his face stole her breath.

This time he went in front of her as he led her down the smooth wooden steps, ready to catch her if she slipped. She was tempted to do exactly that, just to feel those arms around her again, but common sense prevailed. That he hadn't looked her in the eye since they'd descended from the treehouse, hadn't gone unnoticed, and she hazarded a guess he was regretting kissing her.

Probably not half as much as she was regretting kissing him.

Except, she wasn't – not if she was honest with herself. How could anyone regret something so good? She'd felt his passion from the top of her head to the tips of her toes, and it was still surging through her. Her lips continued to tingle and the scent of him lingered in her nose.

They walked back in silence, the friendly easy banter of earlier replaced by awkwardness and the knowledge that what had passed between them couldn't be undone. How could you unkiss someone?

The damage was done, and all she could do now was see if they could move on from it. She hoped they could, because she thoroughly enjoyed his company. Beneath the handsome sexiness, Max was considerate and caring, and plain good fun to be with, and she didn't want to lose that. If their weekly lunches ended, she'd miss them far more than she should, considering he was nothing more than a colleague.

Ah, but he wasn't just a co-worker, was he, her mind whispered, treacherously. And she was forced to admit he wasn't. He'd become much, much more, and she wasn't at all happy about it. Not when she was twenty-eight weeks pregnant. She should be focusing all her attention on the baby, not on romance.

Besides, how could he be interested in her in that way? Not with her growing another man's child in her womb.

So why had he kissed her?

'I expect you would like a rest before dinner,' he said, breaking into her whirling, confused thoughts, and she realised they'd reached the hotel.

Numbly, she nodded, not knowing what she wanted, and then he was gone, leaving her perplexed and more than a little hurt at his abrupt departure.

Cynthia stood uncertainly in reception, her eyes lingering on the door he'd disappeared through, until she became aware of the curious stare of the young lady behind the desk. Giving herself a mental shake, she made her way to her room, and collapsed on the bed, her thoughts a jumbled scattered mess.

What had she done?

She lay there, staring at the ceiling, getting crosser and crosser. For goodness' sake, she told herself – it was a kiss. That was all. Not a declaration of undying love or a marriage proposal. It was a *kiss*. And it wasn't her first one, either. Over the course of her forty-four years, she'd had many. Some good, some not so good. Just because this one had been the best ever, didn't make it life-changing, or anything. It was just a bloody kiss, so she needed to stop being so melodramatic about it.

Moreover, he mightn't have thought it was all that good. Maybe he'd had loads of kisses which had been far better than the one they'd shared. In any case, it probably didn't mean anything to him, so why should it mean anything to her? It had been relief, that's all. He'd thought she was dead or something, and kissing her had been a simple knee-jerk reaction to discovering she was all right and that he wasn't going to be arrested for manslaughter.

Or, and a delicious shiver shot through her, maybe he had been punishing her for tricking him…? If that was the case, she could consider herself well and truly reprimanded. What a punishment – she'd tried to make him think she'd fainted, and he'd made her fall in love with him. If she hadn't been convinced of her feelings for him before, the kiss had sealed it;

she was in love (not lust) with Max Oakland and there wasn't a damned thing she could do about it.

When it was finally time for dinner, Cynthia entered the dining room with a certain degree of trepidation. Not knowing what to expect or how to behave – and not wanting him to realise the extent of her feelings towards him – she'd decided to act as though nothing had happened. Max, it seemed, had taken the exact same stance, and therefore the conversation at dinner was stiff and somewhat strained.

'Hi, did you have a good rest?' he asked when she approached the table he was already seated at. She half-expected him to take her in his arms, but all he did was rise awkwardly to his feet, lean towards her, and give her a chaste kiss on the cheek.

'Yes, thanks.' She took a seat and picked up the menu. What a difference a few hours made, she thought, recalling their far more relaxed lunch, and she hoped this wasn't a predictor of the way it was going to be between them from now on.

Things didn't get any better as the meal progressed though. If anything, the conversation became even more stilted, as Cynthia picked her way through what she supposed was a delicious wild venison cutlet with blackberry chutney and seared spinach, but she hardly tasted any of it.

Dessert suffered the same fate, as she pushed it around her plate wishing she'd never come to Greenleaves in the first place.

She should have followed her instincts and not given in to her attraction to him. It was never a good idea to mix business with pleasure – look what had happened to her the last time she'd done that! Although her baby's father had been pure pleasure with not a hint of business in sight, if she hadn't decided to tag a few days holiday onto a business trip she wouldn't be sitting here now.

And neither would she have a belly full of baby – but that was something she couldn't bring herself to regret. Despite her initial shocked reaction, she wanted this baby more than she'd wanted anything else in her life.

As soon as the meal was over, she made her excuses and retreated to her room, pleading tiredness after a long day. He probably didn't believe her, considering it was only nine p.m. and she was supposed to have had a nap in the afternoon, but she didn't care.

Conscious of his eyes on her as they left the dining room, feeling them on her back like a caress, she had to steel herself not to turn around, march back to the table, and snog him senseless.

Then she let out a snort of derision – she was behaving like a hormone-riddled teenager. *Snog* him, indeed. She didn't do snogging and hadn't done since that memorable encounter with Dizzy Templeton behind the art block in school. Memorable solely because it was the first time a boy had kissed her and she'd fancied him rotten for months. Looking back, it hadn't been terribly good – more like having her mouth attacked by a washing machine on spin. Now that had been a snog; what she wanted to do to Max was as far from a snog as it was possible to get.

She hadn't got undressed yet when there was a knock on the door, and her tummy lurched. She blamed it on the baby (she was doing that a lot, lately) but in her heart she knew it was because she hoped it was Max.

It was.

He was standing there looking nervous and contrite, and so damned sexy she wanted to grab him by the lapels and drag him inside.

Instead, she said, 'Hi.'

'Hi. I… erm… wanted to apologise for earlier. I should never have um…'

'Kissed me?'

'Yeah…' The word came out on the heels of a long sigh.

'You can't take all the blame. I kissed you back.' And it had felt so darned good, so right, as though she had been made to fit into his arms. She licked her lips, remembering the soft firmness of his, and his gaze dropped to her mouth.

When he brought his attention back to her eyes, desire swirled in their depths and she shivered. 'You did, didn't you?' His voice was husky and a tremor of lust flowed over her.

'I still think I should apologise, though,' he continued. 'Taking advantage of a woman when she's down is wrong.'

'I was "down" as you put it, because I had pretended to faint. I wasn't genuinely unwell.'

'I know.'

A door slammed somewhere in the building, and Cynthia jumped. 'Do you want to come in?' Please say you do…

'I'd better not.'

'Oh. OK.' She'd read it wrong; she'd read *him* wrong – she could have sworn he wanted her as much as she wanted him. Hoping she hadn't made a fool of herself, she forced out a smile, praying she looked unconcerned with no hint of the hurt she was feeling.

'It's not that I don't want to, it's just… Oh, hell, I want to make love to you, Cynthia Smart, and if I come into your room, I don't trust myself not to do exactly that.'

And with that astounding declaration, he turned briskly on his heel and was off down the stairs as though a swarm of angry bees were after him.

Shocked, Cynthia slowly closed the door and leant against it, her fingers on her lips, her heart in her mouth. He *did* want her, and the knowledge sent her reeling. As did the realisation he evidently didn't intend to do anything about it.

What was she supposed to do *now*? How was she supposed to feel?

With a shake of her head, she realised she had absolutely no idea. But what he'd just said left such a warm glow in her heart, she prayed it wasn't just sex he wanted. She hoped he was falling for her, too.

Please…

Chapter 25

Milking a cow wasn't Cynthia's idea of fun. Max didn't expect her to do any actual milking herself – they had machines for that – but he did take her to the milking shed, which had one lonely sorrowful looking cow in it, with the largest udder Cynthia had ever seen. Not that she'd seen any others and neither was she too keen on viewing this one, but Max had said over breakfast he wanted her to have the whole field to fridge experience. And the first part involved watching a poor cow being milked.

To be fair to the cow, she didn't seem to mind the process, standing calmly and nosing greedily at a hay net while fearsome-looking metal things were attached to her teats.

Cynthia winced as the machine began to do its job, marvelling at the way the creamy white liquid flowed through the pipe.

'The rest of them have been done,' Max explained. 'I asked Joe to keep one of them back, as I didn't think you'd appreciate getting up at five o'clock this morning for the real thing.'

'Thank you for being so considerate,' she replied, recoiling in horror as the huge cow whose hips were bonier than those belonging to a runway fashion model, decided now would be a good time to produce a cow pat.

'Gross,' she muttered, hoping none of the resultant splatter had landed on her borrowed wellies.

Joe laughed. He was possibly around the same age as her and Max, his pleasant-looking face tanned by wind and sun, laughter lines radiating out from hazel eyes, and a ready smile. 'Farming's a mucky business, to be sure, but it'll be worth it when you get to churn some butter.'

Would it? Cynthia wasn't convinced. She'd be quite happy to accept Max's word that as much food and dairy produce as possible was supplied to the hotel by the adjacent farm. She hadn't felt the need for a practical demonstration, yet here she was in a dirty shed staring at the rear end of an equally dirty cow.

'I must admit, I don't know much about farming,' Cynthia said, meaning she knew nothing at all and wasn't sure she wanted to learn.

'Lara, my wife, was the same when we first met,' Joe said. 'Seeing her first male lamb being castrated was nearly the end of us.'

Cynthia turned her horrified gaze on him. 'I'm not surprised.' God, she hoped she didn't have to witness such an act today. She felt rather sorry for this poor woman; what other horrors had she been forced to endure?

'She was a city girl through and through, but you wouldn't know it now,' he added.

'Are these her wellies, by any chance?'

164

Joe said, 'They are. And she can't wait to meet you.'

'Oh?'

'Max hadn't told us—'

'I think Cynthia has seen enough of the milking,' Max interrupted, giving Joe a strained look.

'Right. OK.' Joe appeared a little put out. 'Um… follow me, and I'll take you through to the pasteurisation room. This pipe here collects the raw milk and it flows into—'

Cynthia zoned out. She was too busy wondering what Joe had been about to say that Max hadn't wanted her to hear, but she was forced to refocus when Joe held out a glass.

'Here's one I prepared earlier,' he joked. 'It's cold, full cream organic milk. See what you think?'

Cynthia took a sip, and then another. 'Mmm, it's so creamy.'

'It is, isn't it? And it makes delicious butter and cheese. Our yoghurts aren't too bad either.'

'They're some of the best in the country,' Max said. 'He's being modest. Every dairy product in both the hotel and the shop is produced here on the farm. Joe also has a herd of goats, and Lara is busy experimenting with goat milk soaps and lotions. When they're ready, we'll sell those in the shop too, as well as using them in the hotel.'

'If you don't mind me asking, how much excess do you produce?' Cynthia wanted to know. 'And do you manage to sell it all?'

Max and Joe swapped glances. 'It depends,' Max said. 'At certain times of the year there is a glut of certain things. We freeze and cold store what we can, pickle and preserve the rest. It has come to the point though, that we have enough darned chutney to last us ten years.'

'It doesn't sell?' she asked.

'It does, but we don't have the footfall to sell it in the quantities we need in order to shift it all. We do have a couple of shelves in the corner shop in the village, but it's not nearly enough, and we supply a couple of local cafes and restaurants.'

Cynthia narrowed her eyes as she thought. 'What about other places around here? This is a tourist spot, for goodness' sake. You'd think there'd be enough visitors to the area.'

'There are, but both the farm and the hotel are all about local mileage only. What we don't want to do, is to increase our carbon footprint by transporting stock all over the place.'

Cynthia frowned. 'You're in London often enough,' she pointed out. 'That amount of travel can't be good for your carbon footprint.'

'I agree. But there are extenuating circumstances.'

'Hmm.' He clearly didn't intend to share the details with her, but she could guess a director's salary must have been extenuating enough to tempt him to get in his car. She didn't blame him, though, because she'd also been seduced by it, and still was.

Conscious of the heat of his gaze on her face, she turned away, pretending to study the gleaming steel contraption which was the pasteurisation machine, and wishing he wouldn't stand so close. She could smell his aftershave, and she was certain she could feel the warmth of his skin. Five feet away was not nearly far enough, not when the temptation to reach out to him was almost overwhelming. Thank goodness Joe was there.

'Have you thought about a collaboration?' she asked, saying something, anything, to take her mind off those soft lips of his.

'With whom?'

'This is just me throwing ideas around, but what about partnering up with a mobile library – not for the refrigerated products, of course – or tagging along on a local meals-on-wheels service? I know it will add to your mileage to get your produce to them in the first place, but you'll also be targeting people who can't get out to the shops easily. A kind of two-birds-with-one-stone thing. Or you could open up the restaurant to the general public and not just paying guests, or maybe have a tea-room, either at the hotel or here. You could run butter-making workshops, or… I don't know… bee-keeping courses. This is just off the top of my head – give me a couple of hours and I'm sure I could come up with loads of other ideas.' She paused for breath to find the two men open-mouthed. 'What?'

'I told you she was good,' Max said to Joe, who nodded.

'There you are!' A woman's voice called out and a figure filled the doorway. 'I'm gasping for a cuppa, but I wanted to wait for Cynthia. What's taking you so long?' The woman stepped forward and held out a hand. 'I'm Lara, Joe's wife. You must be Cynthia?'

Cynthia took her hand and shook it. 'Hi, nice to meet you.'

'Either this pair have been boring you to death, or you have a weird fascination for cows. Come on, let's get acquainted and let the boys play with these hideous lumps of metal.' She turned to leave and Cynthia stepped towards her, gathering the folds of her flowing skirt so it wouldn't brush against the doorframe. A loose dress wasn't the best choice of garment to wear on a farm, but she hadn't realised she'd be tramping around a farmyard or getting up close and personal with livestock.

'I've got—' Lara stopped, her attention on Cynthia's neat bump which was nicely highlighted. Her gaze shot from her to Max and back again. 'I'm sorry, I… um… what was I saying?'

'It's OK, you can ask. Yes, I'm pregnant. Six months, actually. I know how awkward it can be if you congratulate someone on their pregnancy, only for them to say they're not.' Cynthia laughed lightly. Yep, she'd been there and done that on one memorable occasion with someone she hadn't seen since they were at school together. She could still see the woman's indignant expression and feel her own mortification as she realised her mistake.

'Well, I never! Max kept that—' Lara began but Max cut in.

'Lara!' He shook his head and Lara halted.

'Um, right… tea. Or do you prefer coffee?' the woman asked, and although she'd changed the subject willingly enough, Cynthia could tell she was bursting with curiosity.

'Tea, please. I've gone right off coffee.'

'Have you? I did the very same thing with my first. All of a sudden, it tasted hideous, and I'm still not keen on it even now, over five years and another baby later.'

Cynthia glanced back over her shoulder, wondering if Max and Joe were following along behind. They weren't; they were in a deep discussion, but some kind of sixth sense made Max look around at the very same moment, and the expression on his face took her breath away.

For a second, she could have sworn he was looking at her with what could only be described as love in his eyes; then he moved, the light changed, and the expression she'd thought she'd seen had vanished – if it had ever been there in the first place.

'How many do you have?' Cynthia asked, turning her attention back to Lara.

'Two, one of each. Hector is the oldest, he's five and a right scamp, and Kiki is just gone two, and an absolute diva. Their grandma is looking after Kiki today, and Hector has just started school. Six months gone, did you say?'

'Er, yes. Twenty-eight weeks. Nearly twenty-nine.'

'You're so tiny! I was like a hippo with both of mine.' She showed Cynthia into a cosy kitchen with a bright and airy conservatory attached to it. 'Sit down and I'll put the kettle on. I'm sorry I didn't notice you were pregnant at first, and when I did, it took me by surprise.'

'I don't follow.' Cynthia sat down, hoping her borrowed Wellington boots didn't have too much muck on them, and wishing she'd brought her own shoes with her to change into.

'I know Max doesn't want me to talk about it – he made that abundantly clear.' She laughed lightly. 'But he can't expect me not to, not when it's in my face, so to speak.'

'I still don't follow.' Now she was thoroughly confused.

'Max never said you were pregnant. I know it's none of my business, but he and Joe have been friends for a long time, and I can't believe he's not said anything. Never mind, you're here now. How long are you staying?'

'Erm, just until tomorrow—'

'That's a shame, we've got plans tonight, otherwise I'd ask you both to dinner to celebrate. I know you can't have any champagne at the moment, but the farm next door does a mean sparkling apple juice. I bartered some soap for it. You must try my soap! Remind me to give you some before you go. I'm hoping it's good for stretch marks, so you must let me know how you get on with it. Not that I'm suggesting you've got stretch marks, by the way. Listen to me – anyone would think we don't get visitors to the farm very often.'

Lara paused for breath and Cynthia leapt in. 'The baby isn't Max's.'

169

For the first time since Lara had introduced herself, she seemed lost for words.

'And we're not together, either,' Cynthia added for good measure, just in case her new friend had got the wrong end of the stick about that, too.

'Are you sure?' Lara finally asked, a pink spot of colour on each cheek.

'Perfectly sure.' Was she? Or was there a hint of something developing between them that was a little too new and fragile to have a name but was there all the same.

'I could have sworn... I mean, the way he talks about you—'

'Max talks about me?' Her voice rose an octave.

'All good things, honest. He can't stop; it's Cynthia this, and Cynthia that.' She chuckled indulgently. 'And I saw the way he looked at you. I know I was only in the pastuer shed for a minute, but... Oh, hell, I've gone and put my foot in it, haven't I? No wonder Max tried to shut me up.'

Cynthia made a face. 'It was a mistake, that's all.'

'Thank God your husband didn't hear me say that.' Then she must have read Cynthia's expression correctly because she closed her eyes briefly, opened them again and said, 'You're not married, are you?'

'No.'

'Fiancé? Partner? Significant other?'

'No, no and no.'

Lara's mouth snapped shut and she mimed zipping it up. 'I'm not saying another word,' she declared, her voice muffled as she tried to keep her lips from moving, and Cynthia burst out laughing.

170

Lara was such a refreshing change from the guarded world of corporate politics which was her day to day life. The woman said what she was thinking and nothing was meant in a sarcastic or malicious way. She was open and friendly, and Cynthia adored her already. It was a pity she'd probably never see her again after this initial meeting – she would love to have a friend like Lara.

'Max and I are just colleagues,' she said, to put Lara out of her curiosity-fuelled misery. 'We work together, that's all.' She smiled widely. 'I only met him three months ago, so he couldn't possibly be my baby's father.'

'That's such a shame.' Lara couldn't remain silent for long, and those few seconds had obviously been too much for her. 'If anyone is cut out to be a dad, it's Max. He's fantastic with our two. Much better than Joe, if I'm honest. Joe is happy enough to stick his hand up a cow's bottom, but ask him to change a nappy and he goes green at the gills.'

'Is that a thing?'

'Of course it is.' Lara's eyebrows shot up. 'They need changing every couple of hours, especially when they're tiny. I take it, this is your first?'

'And my last, but I was talking about sticking your hand up a cow's bottom.'

'Can we join you?' Joe asked, stomping into the kitchen and leaving a trail of dried mud on the floor in his wake, which made Cynthia feel a little less guilty about still having her wellies on. 'If you want to shove your hand up a cow's backside, I can arrange it for you, but I must say it's not the most pleasant experience you can have.'

'Better than changing a nappy, eh, Joe?' Lara laughed, and Joe pulled a face and shrugged.

Cynthia thought the easy banter between the two was charming, but it was Max who claimed her attention. He was watching Joe and his wife with a soft expression, and was there a hint of wistfulness in it, too?

She wished the men hadn't turned up when they did, because she wanted to ask Lara about Max. There was such a lot she wanted to know, and the first question she would have asked, was what Lara had meant when she said she'd seen the way Max had been looking at her.

Because Cynthia had the strangest feeling she was guilty of looking at him the same way.

Chapter 26

'Lara likes you, and so does Joe,' Max announced at dinner that evening.

'I like them, too,' Cynthia replied. 'How long have they been married?'

'About eight years, although they've been together longer than that. It took Joe a while to convince her to give up her slick city life and go play farmer and wife in the country.'

'They look very happy.'

'They are, they're the happiest couple I know, and they complement each other really well. Joe does all the big, heavy stuff, and Lara is a details person. Joe decides to buy the bull, or the ram, or the new harvester, and Lara reads the small print and does the due diligence. She's also a whizz at churning butter. It's a pity you didn't get to have a go; I'm sure you'd be a natural.'

'I'm not. I prefer inanimate objects like computers to cattle. And that turkey was hideous.' It had stalked across the yard, glaring menacingly at her as they'd left, and she'd felt quite threatened, although Max hadn't been at all bothered. 'Awful looking thing. It's put me off Christmas lunch this year, I can tell you.' Maybe it had been destined for the table but it had escaped being eaten because it was so darned ugly. Who'd want something like that for lunch on Christmas day?

Just then the thought hit her – by the time Christmas came around, she'd have a brand-new baby to take care of. The thought scared her even more than the turkey had. What if she wasn't any good at it? What if the baby didn't like her? Or she developed post-natal depression, or she couldn't cope, or—?

'I had a long chat with Joe this afternoon,' Max said.

'Oh?'

'I know it's not his decision, but I've known him a long time and I value his opinion. He agrees with me.'

'Good, that's great.' She had no idea what he was talking about and wished he'd get on with it. For some reason, Max seemed to be nervous; he was twisting his dark grey napkin into knots. Cynthia preferred stark white table linen, but white meant they were more difficult to keep white, and grey didn't involve having to use harsh chemicals on them every day, he'd informed her.

'So, what are your thoughts?' he asked.

'Hm?'

'You don't have to make a decision now. I'm not desperate. I can wait. I can even wait until after you've had the baby, if necessary.'

What was he talking about? What had she missed when she'd been musing about bloody table napkins? *What had he asked her?*

'Sorry, could you say that again. I'm not sure I heard you correctly.'

He frowned a little, but repeated what he'd said.

It wasn't something she'd been expecting. And it took her completely by surprise.

'I want to offer you a job,' he said.

'A job.' Her response was wooden. Gobsmacked – not a word she would normally use – was the expression which came to mind. Blindsided was another. 'What kind of job?' It had better not involve cow's bottoms, she thought slightly hysterically.

'Operations manager. I'm sorry, I wasn't clear; I know it's a huge step down from what you're doing now, and I can't offer you a directorship, but I can offer you childcare.'

Cynthia shook her head. This was becoming quite surreal. 'Childcare,' she repeated, blankly

'Much of what you will be required to do can be done via remote working. You can access all the files from home, and most of the meetings can be done online, although you may want to come into the office to touch base every now and again. As I said, you don't need to decide immediately. I can't quite match the salary you're on now, but I can get to within two-thirds of it, plus a decent benefits and share package.'

'A job,' she repeated, unable to move past the idea to consider the reality.

'Yes…'

'Here?'

'Yes.'

'Working for you?'

'Is that going to be a problem? Look, if it's about yesterday, then please be assured it won't happen again.' He stopped and

175

focused on the wall behind her and muttered, 'Not unless you want it to.' Then he winced and added in a louder voice, 'I don't mean that in a creepy, stalkerish, the boss is coming onto you way. I meant— Oh, shit, I'm doing a Lara.'

He pulled a face and despite her shock, Cynthia laughed. He looked so adorably sexy she wanted to throw herself across the table.

Instead, she said, 'It's a bit of a shock.'

'I know. Will you be all right?'

She rolled her eyes. 'Of course I'll be all right. I just need to think about it, that's all. To consider my options.'

'Take as much time as you need. Within reason,' he added. 'I'd like an answer by the time the baby is three years old, if possible. I think it's a reasonable length of time to wait.' His smile told her he was joking.

'Three years old? You're daft.' It was the only thing she could think of to say.

'I must be,' she thought she heard him retort, but he was wiping his mouth with one of those grey napkins, so she wasn't sure he had said anything at all.

Once she was back in her room, Cynthia, ever the organised one, set about making a list – on sheep poo notepaper no less. Ew. The thought was horrid, but the paper itself was smooth and didn't smell at all poo-like.

Pros and cons. Thinking about them kept her awake half the night. Thinking about the man who was responsible for her feeling compelled to make those lists in the first place, kept her awake for the other half. Both lists were long ones. Both had their merits and their drawbacks, and although it took her a good few hours, they were as comprehensive as she could make the by the time she'd finished.

But there was one thing that was on both the pro and con list, depending on which way she viewed the situation. And that was Max himself.

It wouldn't be a good idea to work for a man who she found devastatingly attractive, who she was quite probably in love with and whom she had kissed more than once – con list.

She'd be working for a man who she found devastatingly attractive, who she was quite probably in love with and whom she had kissed more than once – pro list.

Could she honestly work for him knowing how she felt about him? On the other hand, could she turn down the job and run the risk of possibly never seeing him again?

She knew which her heart preferred; she knew what her head preferred.

It was now a question of which one would rule her.

Chapter 27

The following morning, they drove back in relative silence, with Cynthia none the wiser which way she was going to go when it came to making a decision regarding Max's job offer. Ironically, she did know what she would do if she wasn't half in love (only *half?*) with him, and she knew she would have jumped at the chance. But because her heart was involved she didn't know what to do for the best.

Tired and irritable from far too little sleep, she slumped grumpily in the passenger seat. Every now and again the baby would turn, like a tumbling acrobat, making her feel rather queasy. It looked like her daughter was just as grumpy as she was and was making her feelings known.

Did its mother's mood or state of mind have an effect on the baby in the womb, she pondered, trying to think of anything other than the man sitting silently beside her, who was also lost in his own thoughts. She was also beginning to wonder if he was regretting the offer.

178

Or was he simply being quiet in order to give her space to think, and not crowd her?

As she became increasingly more bad-tempered, she found she was gradually coming to resent him for making the offer in the first place, despite the fact it would be the answer to all her problems. If she did take him up on it, she wasn't sure about where she would live, but as she could work mostly from home, then maybe she could remain in London for the time being.

That she didn't want to continue to live in the city, was a whole other matter and a whole other decision. She kept seeing Lara's cosy farmhouse kitchen and the countryside through the farmhouse window, and her thoughts kept returning to her mum's cottage, too. No pollution (apart from smelly cows), no noise (birdsong and bleating sheep didn't count), no crowds. Just wide open spaces for children to explore.

'Grrr.'

'Did you say something?' he asked, his attention on the road, which was incredibly busy this time on a Tuesday morning. If they weren't careful, she'd be late for her appointment.

'Nope.' She shook her head, annoyed with herself for letting her frustration show. He was probably thinking his offer was a no-brainer and was wondering what was holding her back from accepting it. But that was one conversation she seriously wasn't going to have with him. It was bad enough they'd kissed, that her passion had matched his – he didn't need to know she'd lost her heart to him along with her common sense.

Finally, Max aimed the car at a space in the hospital car park and Cynthia sighed with relief. Being cooped up with him in such close proximity for the past two hours had been nothing short of torture, and she was glad to be able to put a little distance between them, even if it was only a couple of feet.

Why she had to have all her antenatal appointments at the hospital was another thing which annoyed her this morning; it was something to do with her being an elderly first-time mum (elderly, indeed! – the cheek of it), and when Max made no move to get out of the car, she huffed loudly.

Thank God, he was staying put, she thought.

Unfortunately, he must have interpreted her relief as disappointment, because she heard the car door slam and his footsteps hurrying to catch up with her as she stomped across the car park.

'Do you want me to come in with you?' he asked, when he fell into step beside her.

'If you want.' It was too late to say no now; they were almost inside the building. To send him back to the car would be churlish.

The fact that she quite liked the idea of having someone with her for once, was neither here nor there. It had no bearing on it. None whatsoever. She was perfectly capable of attending these things on her own, and she had done for all the others. She was simply being polite and not causing a fuss. That was all.

Sitting in the waiting room was a decidedly odd experience with Max by her side. Realising everyone would assume he was the baby's father, she almost felt proud he was there, as if she had her own special someone to share this moment with. It was only a routine appointment, no scan scheduled, but nevertheless it felt good to have him by her side.

'Ms Smart?' A nurse with a clipboard scanned the room and Cynthia stood up. 'Are you coming, too, dad?' the woman asked, looking brightly at Max. Yes, Cynthia was right – the nurse had assumed he was her baby's father.

Max got to his feet. It looked like he was going all the way with this, and not sitting the actual appointment out in the waiting room.

Strange. But OK. If he didn't mind, then she didn't.

Neither of them bothered to correct the nurse as to the nature of Max's relationship to the baby. Cynthia, for one, didn't feel it was necessary.

Her midwife, Jess, also assumed the same thing as she said to him, 'It's great you could come along. Many dads aren't able to. They manage the scans, but these in between appointments are often missed. I bet you're excited.'

Max smiled vaguely and looked to Cynthia – it was up to her to put Jess right, but once again, she failed to say anything. As soon as the midwife turned away, Cynthia shrugged, hoping Max would interpret the movement as her not being bothered enough to do anything about Jess's misconception, when in fact she was rather enjoying the idea.

'Right then, dad, if you could sit over here while I weigh mum and measure her tummy.' The midwife pointed to a chair and Max dutifully sat.

He looked anywhere other than at Cynthia, and she got the impression he was embarrassed. Unsure whether it was because Jess had assumed he was the father, or whether he was about to watch her being weighed, measured and other assorted intimate things, she simply couldn't tell.

'His name is Max,' she said to Jess, 'and he's not the baby's father – he's a friend.'

'Nice to meet you, Max,' Jess replied brightly. 'OK, then, let's get started. Cynthia, would you like to get on the scales?'

Cynthia most certainly wouldn't, but she did as she was told, averting her eyes from the resultant number on the display. She wasn't huge, but she felt it, and she didn't need any reminders of how much weight she'd have to lose once the baby was here.

Next, Jess used a tape measure around her bump and recorded that figure, too, and then she took Cynthia's blood pressure.

'It's a little high,' the midwife said, 'but nothing to worry about at the moment. I'd like to keep an eye on it, though, so I want to see you again in two weeks.'

After the urine test, which was clear (Cynthia blushed when she handed over a little bottle of pee), Jess said they were done. 'At your next appointment we'll have a chat about your plans for the birth, your expectations, and your options. Have you been attending parentcraft classes?'

'Erm, no, not yet.'

'You might want to – they can be helpful, especially when it comes to the actual birth and the first few weeks afterwards. How are baby's movements?'

'She's lively,' Cynthia reported with a grimace. 'More so during the night.'

'That's nature's way of preparing you for all those midnight feeds,' Jess joked. 'Talking of feeds, have you decided to bottle or breastfeed? We do encourage mums to breastfeed, especially in the first few weeks and months, because it's best for your baby, so give it some thought.'

Cynthia bit her lip. Yet one more thing to add to the pro list for accepting Max's job offer. Breastfeeding and going back to work full time would be difficult, and she wanted to do what was best for her child.

'OK, do you have any questions?' Jess asked.

Cynthia shook her head.

'Max? I know you're not the baby's father, but have you got anything you'd like to ask me? Maybe something Cynthia might have forgotten?'

'I don't think so,' he said, looking even more uncomfortable than he had earlier, if that was at all possible.

'Great. Don't forget to make an appointment on the way out. And if you have any concerns, no matter how small or how silly you think they are, you have my phone number. Take care and I want to see your blood pressure down a bit next time.'

Cynthia promised she'd try her best and left, Max opening the door for her to let her leave first. As she stepped through, she heard him say to Jess, 'I'll make sure her blood pressure is down,' and the grumpiness which had mostly receded came flying back with a vengeance.

'How dare you!' she said, rounding on him once they were clear of the building and heading towards the car park. 'You're not responsible for me. I can take care of myself, thank you very much – I don't need you to do it for me.'

'I know, but I am your friend – if you'd let me be – and if I can help in any way, shape, or form, I will.'

'I don't need your help,' she retorted angrily, yanking the car door open.

'Does that mean you're turning my offer of a job down?'

'No, it does not. It means I'm still thinking about it.' She crossed her arms, folding them resolutely above her bump and glaring through the windscreen.

'Good. I'm glad.' He started the car and drove towards the main road, Cynthia quietly seething.

If she was asked, she would say it was because it was presumptuous of him to tell Jess he'd make sure her blood pressure was lower for her next appointment. If she was honest with herself, the real reason she was cross was because for a moment or two she'd loved pretending he was her baby's father. And she also would have liked him to have contradicted her when she introduced him as her friend.

Was that all he was? All he considered himself to be?

Suddenly, her ire dissolved, to be replaced by desolation and incredible sadness.

Serve her right for kissing him.

She'd gone and got her heart broken and she still didn't know what to do about the blimmin' job.

Chapter 28

Cynthia knew she had scared Max off. It wasn't surprising. After he'd dropped her at the office, he had driven away and she hadn't seen hide nor hair of him since. For two long weeks she'd expected some contact, even if it was only a text. He wasn't in the office, and neither had he been in touch about their weekly lunch date (*date*? hah! she wished). She'd half expected him to turn up for her latest antenatal appointment (blood pressure down a bit, thank goodness). Nothing.

She'd been tempted to question Sally, because her PA knew everything. She hadn't though, not wanting to appear to care. Although she did care, very much indeed.

How can a guy kiss you, offer you a job, promise to look after you (aka make sure your blood pressure didn't blow the top of your head off), then disappear off the face of the earth. It only proved he hadn't been thinking along the same lines as her at all. The kiss had been just that. Nothing more. She suspected he was avoiding her because he regretted it.

She was bitterly regretting it, too. What an incredibly daft thing to do.

Oh, but it had been soooo good. She hadn't felt so alive in… forever. Not even during her mad passionate midlife fling with Stan. And look how that had turned out. She should have been satisfied with the car as a nod to her midlife crisis, but she couldn't bring herself to regret conceiving little Myrtle, or Felicity. She hadn't decided on a name yet, but Hannah was definitely in the running.

And thinking about her car got her to thinking she must part exchange it for something more baby-friendly soon. She could hardly get a postage stamp in the boot (remember them?) let alone a pram, shopping, and the baby itself. Not that the baby would go in the boot – but she had a feeling a car seat probably wouldn't fit in the passenger seat of her slick little sports car.

Time for another list.

Cynthia opened the spreadsheet she'd begun when she first discovered she was pregnant and created a new page, calling it "car swap".

She then spent the following forty-five minutes on various car sales sites, looking for something suitable. A tank would be ideal (less chance of anyone, ie, the baby, getting hurt if she was driving one of those) but failing that, the next best thing would do. If she could afford it.

She should obtain a decent amount for her sporty number – it was less than a year old – but she was realistic enough to understand the value would have dropped the second she'd driven it off the forecourt.

Great; yet another expense, and she still hadn't bought the big stuff yet, like a pram or a cot. And looking at the prices of those items, it was enough to send her blood pressure soaring again. Babies were *spendy*.

A tap on her office door made her quickly shut down the site she'd been gazing at which had the cutest crib she'd ever seen, and bring up the document she was supposed to be working on. Sally must be at lunch, or else she'd have acted as gatekeeper and would have given her fair warning. At least she knew it wasn't Ricky (Ricky who? she'd not clapped eyes on him since he'd booted her off the Field Mouse Project) because he never knocked. Barge right on in was his preferred method and even Sally, with her Rottweiler tendencies, couldn't waylay him.

'Come in,' she called, keeping her attention on her screen, as if she was too busy to be interrupted.

'We need to talk,' Max said.

Oh, hell, she wasn't prepared for this. Her heart missed a beat, then did a double-thump thing to make up for it, causing her to wince. 'About what?'

That's the way, she said to herself. Keep it cool and he'd never know how flustered she was feeling right now. Although the warmth spreading into her face might just give her away. And she needed to pee. Again. Which was making her squirm in her chair.

'I know I said you could take as much time as you need – and that still stands – but my head is all over the place, and it's your fault,' Max announced.

'Mine?' It came out as a squeak and she cleared her throat.

'Yes, yours. I came here to apologise for the way I acted, but I can't.'

'Apologise for what?' she said, before realising it sounded as though she didn't think he had anything to apologise for. He didn't. She was to blame just as much as him; if she hadn't pretended to pass out, then he wouldn't have scooped her up in his arms and—

'For assuming I could step in and make you slow down.'

Eh? Oh, he was talking about the comment he'd made to her midwife. Not the kissing thing.

Interesting.

The baby kicked her in the ribs, directly underneath her heart, and she inhaled sharply. Or that was the reason she told herself for her heart doing the jitterbug in her chest. Not the fact that he didn't regret kissing her and she was inordinately pleased he didn't.

'What about…?' she asked, kicking herself as the words tripped over her lips without her brain checking out what she was going to say first.

'What?'

'Never mind.'

'Are you worried about the baby?'

'The baby is fine. We both are.'

'I mean, when he or she arrives. I was serious when I said you can mostly work from home, and when you need to come to Greenleaves, you can bring the baby with you. There may be the odd meeting off-site, but I'm sure we can work something out.'

'You want me that badly, eh?' she joked, then almost did pass out for real when his intense expression seared her.

'Yes.'

'Oh. OK. I… um…'

'I'm sorry, I shouldn't have come. I did say I'd give you all the time you needed, and here I am, hassling you.'

'I like being hassled.'

'You do?'

'By you.'

Ah.' His smile was slow to start, but by the time it got going it had spread right across his face.

She adored the way his eyes crinkled at the corners. She adored the way he made her feel like she was the most important thing in his world right now. And she sincerely hoped that was true.

'I'll let you know tomorrow,' she promised.

'You will?'

She nodded. Her head might be all over the place, but she had to decide one way or the other. Whichever way she decided to go, arrangements had to be made. Lots of them.

Her gaze remained fixed on the doorway after he left, and she abruptly felt utterly exhausted. She needed to visit the loo more than ever, but she was too knackered to move. Besides, her boobs were tender, she ached in places she'd never ached before, and now she could add heartburn to her list of woes.

But none of it mattered.

Inside her head, she was dancing on tables and singing at the top of her voice.

She'd made her decision – she would accept his offer, but they would have to clear the air first. Set out boundaries. Make sure they both knew where they were going. If she was to do this, to make such a momentous move, it would have to be because it was the sensible thing to do. Not because her heart and her nether regions thought it was a good idea. Her acceptance would have to be based on logic, and not on the vague hope he felt the same way about her as she did about him, and maybe, possibly, sometime in the future they might get together.

She'd have to make it clear – there would be no getting together. If she put her feelings for him to one side, she acknowledged he was a good man, a decent guy, and she'd have to be content to love him from afar.

Because this decision wasn't solely about her, about her needs and wants – it was about what was best for her baby. However good the establishment was, having a mother around was far better for the child than being in a nursery for ten hours a day.

And not only that, Cynthia made another decision too – one she needed to speak to her mum about before she acted on it.

'Mum? It's me.'

'Is everything all right?'

'It's fine – more than fine. I want to run something by you. Please don't feel you have to say yes right away, or at all for that matter. I'll understand if you say no. It's a big ask and—'

'Yes.'

'You don't know what I'm going to say?'

'I know you almost as well as you know yourself, Cynthia Jane Smart. And the answer is yes, you can come and stay as long as you like. I hate the thought of you having the baby in London, with no one to care for you.'

'Mum, it might be for longer than you think. I've been offered a job at Greenleaves, Max's hotel.'

'That's wonderful news!' There was a pause, then her mum said in a rush, 'Are you and Max—?'

'No. We are not,' Cynthia jumped in. But that kiss…? 'And I don't want you thinking we will be. This is a business proposition. Nothing more.'

'Oh, that's a pity. You looked good together, and I still think he fancies the pants off you.'

'Mum! He does not.'

'Hmm.' Her mother changed the subject. 'When are you planning on coming?'

'I'm thirty weeks now, and I'm going to work until I'm thirty-nine weeks. That will give me as long as possible on maternity leave.'

'Don't work too long, will you dear. Carrying a baby is exhausting, and you're only going to get bigger. Do you want me to register you with my GP? And how about if I get a man in to decorate your bedroom?'

'Great, that'll be wonderful. And, Mum? I do love you, you know.'

'I know. Take care of yourself and my grandchild. Ooh, I can't wait!'

Cynthia was still grinning broadly when Sally stuck her head around the door a half an hour later to see if she wanted tea.

'You look happy,' her PA noted.

'I suppose I am.'

'Any particular reason? A certain handsome one?'

Cynthia gave her a Mona Lisa smile. She would have loved to share her news with her PA, but she needed to resign first. It wouldn't be professional to let Sally know her plans before sharing them with Ricky.

As she sat in her office, she understood this life was no longer for her, and a brand new exciting one beckoned.

With quiet joy in her heart she vowed to tell Max tomorrow, and the little baby inside her kicked in agreement.

Chapter 29

'You'll never guess.' Sally stood in the doorway the following morning as Cynthia arrived for work. Her expression was grave.

'What?' Cynthia hung her coat on the stand in the corner, the one she'd got from Portobello Road when she'd climbed far enough up the corporate ladder to be given an office of her own. It was the middle of September and the Indian summer weather London had been enjoying had given way to biting winds and overcast skies. Tomorrow she might consider breaking out the thermal underwear.

Sally was wringing her hands and shuffling nervously. Whatever news she had, she didn't look too happy about sharing it.

A cold shiver made the hairs on the back of Cynthia's neck prickle – what she was about to hear wasn't going to be good.

'It's about Max,' Sally said.

'Go on,' Cynthia urged, cautiously. Please don't tell me anything has happened to him, she prayed. She slowly sank into her chair, dread washing over her.

'Mr Webber is his father.' Sally stopped shuffling about and was twisting the chain on her necklace, and studying her with concern.

Cynthia stared at her PA, her mind oddly blank. For some reason, she thought she had said—

'He's Mr Webber's son.' Sally clarified, and bit her lip, her brow creased by worry. 'Are you OK?'

What the—? It couldn't possibly be true. Could it? Cynthia most definitely wasn't OK. She was as far from OK as it was possible to get. 'I'm fine,' she replied, her tone falsely bright.

'Can I get you anything? Tea? Water?'

How about a surgeon to remove the bloody great knife wedged between her shoulder blades? 'No thanks, I'm fine,' she repeated, resolutely.

'Are you sure?'

She nodded. Her head felt as though it was bobbing up and down like one of those nodding dogs she remembered seeing on the parcel shelves of cars when she was a child. Nod, nod, nod.

She forced herself to stop – her head would drop off if she carried on.

'Is there anything else?' she added. She tried out a smile to show Sally she was OK; it felt more like a grimace.

Her PA hesitated.

'Go on, spill. In for a penny, in for a pound.' Her smile stayed in place, but inside a scream was beginning to build. He was Ricky's *son*? How the hell—? She had been going to tell him her decision today. What a fool she was.

'Mr Webber has brought Max on board because... well... his kids. The legitimate ones. You know how useless he thinks they are?'

Cynthia knew, all right. Which was why she'd had such high hopes of being the CEO one day. It looked like those had been based on falsehoods and lies.

Max should have told her.

She'd fallen in love with him, for God's sake – *he should have told her.*

Sally hadn't finished. 'Mr Webber—'

Cynthia held up a hand. 'No. Please. I don't want to hear anymore.' A thought occurred to her. 'How do you know?'

'Angela told me.'

Cynthia's brows shot up. 'Is it common knowledge?' Did everyone know except her? Angela had been Ricky's PA for years – she knew all about discretion – and she'd hardly have spilt the beans if it wasn't.

'Not yet, but it soon will be. Mr Webber has given Angela her notice.'

'Why?'

'Something to do with a mislaid folder. She's going to fight it, of course, but from outside the company.'

'What an utter bastard,' Cynthia muttered, but she wasn't totally clear whether she was referring to Ricky or his son.

'No one's job is safe,' Sally was saying, wringing her hands. 'If he can do that to Angela, then what will he do to the rest of us?'

What, indeed...

With Ricky, loyalty didn't count, that much was obvious. 'I hope Angela takes him to the cleaners,' she said. She felt like doing the same thing herself.

She also felt like confronting Max.

And that was exactly what she was going to do. It might cost her her job, but she was too upset and too mad to care.

How dare he make such a fool out of her!

Stomping down the corridor, she prayed he was in his office – *Jeff's office*, she corrected herself. Look how quickly Ricky and Max had ousted the poor bloke. They couldn't wait to get rid of him. She'd given Max the benefit of the doubt, blaming it all on the Pitbull, but now she wasn't so sure. Like father, like son, eh Max? He was clearly as ruthless as his dad, and twice as sneaky. At least you knew where you stood with Ricky; he didn't sugar-coat things or hide behind a veneer of friendliness.

Anger bubbled and boiled, and she clung to it. It was the only thing keeping her going. Once it was reduced to a simmer, she had a terrible suspicion all she'd be left with was a broken heart and shattered dreams, so she clung to her rage as desperately as a drowning man clung to a life raft, fearing once she let go of it, heartbreak would overwhelm her.

She slammed into his office, barging through the door, and Max looked up, startled. His welcoming smile slid off his face when he saw her expression.

'What's wrong?' he asked, jumping to his feet. 'Is the baby OK?'

'What do you care, you slimy, sly, underhand, miserable excuse for a man.'

'Pardon?'

'You heard. I can't believe you didn't tell me. What were you waiting for? Me to hand in my resignation? Well, that's not going to happen. If you want to get rid of me, you'll have to sack me, and you can tell your bloody father pregnancy is not a valid reason.'

'Ricky doesn't want to get rid of you.'

'You can drop the pretence; "Dad" will suffice.'

'I've never called him "Dad" and I don't intend to start now. Is that what this is all about? That Ricky is my father?'

'It's enough, isn't it? Or have you got more nasty little secrets you'd like to share?'

He had the grace to look sheepish, and she shook her head in disgust.

'I can't believe I nearly fell for it,' she said, ignoring the fact she *had* fallen – hard – for his offer of a new life and for him. 'You know where you can stick your job. Both of them, because if you think I'm working for you when Ricky hangs up his hand-made briefcase, you've got another think coming.'

She was aware she wasn't making any sense, but she was too angry to think straight.

'I won't be taking over from Ricky. Look, Cynthia, you've got it all wrong—'

'Don't patronise me.'

'I'm not. If you just let me explain—'

'Don't bother, I—'

Cynthia!'

His shout made her jump and her mouth closed with a snap.

'Remember I told you Ricky had made me an offer I couldn't refuse?' He carried on before she was able to speak again. 'He promised to invest in a new Greenleaves hotel with no strings attached if I came to work for him for six months. It was too good an opportunity to pass up.' He held up a hand when she attempted to speak. 'Hear me out, please. Then if you want to continue calling me all the rude names under the sun, be my guest. Ricky hoped when he got me on board – literally, because Jeff became ill and a place on the board opened up – he hoped once I was in, I wouldn't be able to walk away.'

Max paused and Cynthia waited for him to continue. 'He was wrong. I *am* walking away, and I don't want his investment either. I've seen the way he operates and I don't like it. The Field Mouse Project was just another way for him to get his claws into me. He shared a vision with me, in the hope it would persuade me to stay. It didn't. I don't want anything to do with his company.'

'What about him? Ricky?' As Max had been talking, Cynthia realised the fight had drained out of her, leaving her feeling shaky and rather unwell.

She desperately wanted to sit down, but she remained where she was, ready for a swift exit.

'He may be my father, but that doesn't mean I have to like him,' Max said. 'Are you all right? You don't look too good.'

She didn't feel it. As the seconds ticked by, she felt even more unwell. Her heart was thumping erratically and she felt a bit breathless.

'Come here and sit down before you fall down. Let me get you a glass of water.' Max stepped towards her and gently grasped her elbow.

She let him lead her to a chair and she lowered herself carefully into it. There was a dull ache in her back and her legs were wobbly. A wave of weakness washed over her, and she was starting to feel very odd indeed, and decidedly ill.

A sudden sharp pain low down in her abdomen made her cry out and Max dropped to his knees to kneel beside her.

'Cynthia, what's wrong?'

She turned her stricken gaze to him, and the panic on her face was reflected in his eyes.

Please, no, not yet, it's too early, too soon…

A wave of dizziness washed over her, nausea following swiftly behind. A headache was starting to build behind her eyes, and there was another sharp pain just below her ribs.

Dear God, no!

'I think I'm losing the baby,' she cried and burst into tears.

Chapter 30

Thirty weeks was too early. Far too early. She wasn't ready – neither of them were.

'Is she….?' Cynthia's voice was small and she heard the fear in it.

The doctor was staring intently at a computer screen. 'Your midwife noted that at one of your appointments your blood pressure was up, but there was no protein in the urine,' he said. 'Nurse, can we get a protein test done asap?'

A passing nurse stuck her head into the cubicle and nodded.

'What is it?' Cynthia asked. 'What's wrong?'

'Pre-eclampsia, by the look of things. Let's get a foetal monitor on you.'

Within minutes she was wired up with a couple of straps around her bump.

She held her breath and chewed at her lip. Thankfully, the awful sharp pain hadn't been repeated, but that didn't mean to say she wasn't terrified she was in early labour.

'Foetal heart rate is 150,' the doctor informed her.

'Is that bad?'

'It's within the acceptable range.'

'Oh.' She gathered her courage 'Am I losing her?'

'There's no indication you're in early labour.' The doctor patted her on the shoulder.

'Thank God.' Cynthia closed her eyes for a second and breathed deeply. Max's sigh of relief echoed her own.

The nurse returned with a cardboard receptacle. 'I know it's a bit of an awkward position, but try to pee into this.'

Cynthia frowned. She'd do it, of course she would, but not with Max in the cubicle. It was bad enough she had her top hitched up around her boobs and her maternity trousers and pants pulled down to her pubic bone, without him seeing her do that.

He caught her expression. 'I'll just be outside.'

'You don't have to go,' the nurse said. 'You'll see worse than this by the time the baby is born.'

'Yes, he does, and no, he won't,' Cynthia said. 'Out, please. And thank you for calling an ambulance.' This last was aimed at Max.

'I'll wait until you know what's happening.'

'Don't bother.'

'But—'

The nurse interrupted. 'Sorry, my lovely,' she said to Cynthia, 'but I need you to do a sample for me now.'

Cynthia glared at him.

'I'll be outside,' he muttered.

She watched him go, then the nurse pulled the curtain closed and helped her do what was necessary.

Once again there was the excruciating wait for the result, and all the while she was aware of the nurse's curiosity. Consoling herself with the fact the hospital staff probably witnessed far worse than her own little drama, nevertheless she had to say something to explain herself.

'He's a colleague, that's all,' she said.

'There's a trace of protein in your urine,' the doctor informed her before the nurse had a chance to say anything, and the woman gave her a sympathetic smile as she swished the curtain to one side and disappeared through it.

Cynthia felt tears threatening once more. 'What does that mean?'

'You've got mild pre-eclampsia.'

'Is it treatable?'

'The only sure way is to deliver your baby, but that's not an option we would consider at this stage. What I would suggest is rest – not bed rest; I'd like you to keep moving to reduce the risk of blood clots – plenty of fluids, and close monitoring of your blood pressure, every other day in the first instance.'

'But the baby is all right?'

'Yes.'

She relaxed onto the hard trolley. 'That's all that matters.'

'I'll write this up and send it to your midwife and GP. You can have your blood pressure monitored at your local surgery. You'll only need to come to the hospital if there are further concerns. I'm pleased to say your blood pressure has come down a bit since you arrived, so we'll monitor you and baby for a while longer, then if nothing changes you can go home. Remember what I said, though – nothing too strenuous and try to relax. Meditation is good. Do you have anything you'd like to ask me?'

'Do you think stress could have caused it?'

'Possibly. It certainly wouldn't have helped, although some women develop pre-eclampsia for no reason we can determine.'

'Am I OK to go back to work?'

The doctor's expression was sombre. 'I'd prefer it if you didn't. Not for a couple of weeks, at least. Ideally, I'd like to see no protein markers in your urine and your blood pressure lower than it is currently, before you return to your normal activities, and that includes work. I'll sign you off for now, and we'll see how it goes.'

By "we" she knew he was referring to the medical profession as a whole, because the likelihood of seeing this particular doctor again was slim, so she thanked him profusely, then lay back and tried to rest.

It wasn't easy when there was so much going on in her head, but she focused her attention on the numbers on the screen, watching the fluctuating evidence her baby was alive and well.

'Ouch! That hurt.' A solid kick (or it might have been a knee or an elbow, it was difficult to tell) made her wince.

Yet again, tears threatened, as much from relief as from the pain of Max's betrayal. She hoped he wasn't stubbornly waiting for her, because she couldn't face him right now. She wasn't sure she could face anyone. Fortunately (or unfortunately – whichever way she wanted to look at it) there was no one else she had to face. Apart from her mum, she had no one else in her life who'd give two hoots about her. Maybe Ricky would, but that would only be because she wasn't sitting at her desk doing what he was paying her to do.

How sad was that?

This is what her life had become, and she didn't like it one bit.

Taking a shaky breath, she reached for her phone and dialled a familiar number, whispering, 'It'll be OK little one,' to her baby as she waited for it to be answered, and wondering who she was trying to convince.

'Hi, Mum? Can I come home…?'

Chapter 31

It might be the end of September, but the warmth of summer lingered on in clear azure skies and suntraps in sheltered places. It might be a little cool to sit out in the garden to eat breakfast at this time of the morning though, but Cynthia had suffered yet another restless night having been awake for most of it, and had retreated to the garden so as not to wake her mum.

She'd taken a pot of tea out with her (the tea cosy in the shape of a cake never failed to make her smile) and spent a quiet half hour listening to the world coming alive around her.

Dawn, she frequently observed now she had the time to enjoy it and wasn't dashing to work, was her favourite time of day, when everything was new and fresh and nothing ached as much as it did later on in the day.

At thirty-two weeks, her neat little bump had expanded. If she thought she'd felt like a whale before, she hadn't known what was about to hit her, and she anticipated things would get significantly worse before her little one entered the world. Her boobs had grown apace, and were now leaking, which was gross. And she didn't want to think about the haemorrhoid situation (even more gross). Her ankles were slightly swollen, her legs kept cramping and her sleep was all over the place; she was often awake half the night and napping during the day. It was ridiculous.

More out of habit than anything else, Cynthia checked her phone.

No messages, no texts, no emails.

She didn't expect there to be, considering she'd blocked Max's number, but she checked anyway. She had sent him one brief text to say she and the baby were OK, and she was taking some time off work, and please could he respect her wishes and not contact her again. Then she'd blocked him.

Two weeks ago at the hospital, after the doctor had told her she could go, she'd slipped off home, leaving the building by a different exit, and had taken a taxi to the office, where she'd handed Sally the doctor's note and had grabbed her coat and bag. Once she'd arrived home, she'd quickly packed a case, had squashed herself into her car and had driven to her mum's. And there she'd stayed, hiding out for the past two weeks, nursing her broken heart and willing her blood pressure to drop.

The only person from London who she was in regular contact with was Sally, and even that was infrequent, because whether it was subconscious or not (shooting the messenger and all that) Cynthia was reluctant to speak to her PA. It mightn't be fair, but she couldn't help it. She was trying desperately to forget about work and its associations for the duration, and if it meant she hurt Sally's feelings, then so be it.

Cynthia was hurting, too. More than she'd ever thought possible. No man had come anywhere close to penetrating her heart until Max had come along, and he'd not only pierced it, he'd broken it into so many pieces she didn't think it would ever mend.

The only thing keeping her going was the squirming baby inside her and the steady unwavering love of her mother. Her mum didn't know the full story. Cynthia had only shared the briefest of details about her relationship with Max, instead focusing on her health and that of her baby as being the reason she wanted to stay with her. Her mother didn't need to know the truth just yet. There was time enough to let her know she wouldn't be taking the job with Max, but until she'd decided what the alternative was going to be, she was staying silent because her mum would only fret.

Pushing her worries to the back of her mind, Cynthia gave her attention to the present. She was trying to live more in the here and now, to be more mindful, and she noticed that after the initial dawn chorus, the birds settled down and peace descended on the garden, broken only by the distant barking of a dog and the rumble of the occasional car.

Which reminded her, today she had to take her car in for a service. Once that was done, she planned on part-exchanging it. She had no idea what she was going to exchange it for, but she had to begin looking. There were only eight weeks to go before the baby arrived and, if anything, she was even less prepared than she'd been before she'd fled to her mum. However, she couldn't stay here forever, and it would soon be time for her to return to London and sort out her apartment, her job, and her life.

After making the decision to leave the Webber Corporation and Ricky, and bring her child up in the countryside, she didn't want to alter it, but for the present there was nothing else on the horizon when it came to jobs. She could hardly apply for another one right now – one look at her huge belly and the interview would soon be over. So she planned on living in her apartment for the time being, and using her maternity leave to search for another position. There was so much to do she didn't know where to start and had been putting it off, especially with the health scare she'd had. But the monitoring (her mum's GP was very thorough) hadn't thrown up any more issues, so as long as she took it easy and didn't overdo things, going back to work for the remainder of her pregnancy shouldn't be a problem.

Her mum wouldn't be too keen on the idea, of course. It was obvious she was thoroughly enjoying having Cynthia stay, but the situation was unsustainable in the long term. Her mum was too old for such upheaval, and both of them were far too used to their independence.

'You're up early,' Maggie said, wandering onto the patio in her nightie and dressing gown. 'Is there any more tea in the pot?'

'It'll be cold by now. Let me make another.'

'I'll do it, you stay put.'

'I'm perfectly capable of making a pot of tea.'

'I know you are,' her mum replied, her voice carrying a soothing tone. 'But I like to fuss over you.'

And that was half the problem; Cynthia didn't do fussing. She'd enjoyed it for the first few days, with the shock of Max's betrayal and the threat of pre-eclampsia consuming her every thought and leaving her reeling. Her mum had made her endless cups of tea, and had cooked meals she'd barely tasted but had eaten because she knew she had to keep her strength up for the baby's sake. Maggie had fetched her cushions, had curtailed her social calendar so as to be with her, and had asked her what she wanted to watch on TV. She'd made Cynthia an appointment with her own GP, had bought new curtains and bed linen for her old room (although she couldn't do anything about the wallpaper, but once again she had offered to get a man in), and had generally treated Cynthia like she was made of glass and could break at any moment.

Mums weren't stupid and her own knew there was something more going on than high blood pressure (although that was serious enough). But, bless her, she hadn't asked, although she had dropped the occasional unsubtle hint to try to get Cynthia to open up.

'Shall I pop some bread in the toaster?' Maggie asked and Cynthia nodded.

Sitting out here with a cup of tea and hot buttered toast slathered in strawberry jam was fast becoming one of her most favourite things to do.

The two of them ate their breakfasts and discussed their plans for the day.

'I've got to take the car to the garage for a service,' Cynthia said. 'Is there anything you need while I'm out?'

'You could pick up a bag of self-raising flour. I'm going to bake a cake for the Harvest Festival.'

'OK. And what if I get a crusty loaf to have with the soup you made yesterday?'

'Good idea. We can break chunks off and dip them in.' Her mum's eyes lit up and Cynthia smiled to herself. It didn't take much to make her mother happy – she was a cup-half-full person and seemed to take pleasure in almost everything she did. How had Cynthia forgotten that about her?

Spending time with her mum was the one good thing to have come out of the events of two weeks ago. With her living in London and her mum in Little Milling, she supposed it was inevitable they grew apart. And she was always so busy that visits had been fleeting things, fitted in as and when she could manage them.

Now though, she felt she was getting to know her mother all over again, gelling the woman she remembered from her childhood and teenage years with the woman her mum was now. She was very grateful she had been given the time to do that, and she vowed not to let things slip back to the way they had been before. Her mum deserved to get to know her grandchild properly, and not just see her during hastily snatched visits once a month.

Taking her time (there was no need to rush anywhere, and this slower pace of life suited her just fine) Cynthia showered, got dressed, and drove to the garage, which was situated on the edge of the village. She intended to enjoy the walk back, but before she began her leisurely stroll she was going to browse in a shop or two, then treat herself to a cup of tea and a slice of cake in the café attached to the bakery.

There was one thing she hadn't factored in, though. The problem and the joy of village life was everyone knew everyone else and their business, and if they didn't, they soon made it their mission to find out.

It began in the garage.

'You're Maggie's daughter,' the owner said, wiping his hands on a dirty rag.

'That's right.'

'Staying long?'

'Probably not.'

'I remember you from school.'

'Do you?' She didn't remember him. She did, however, remember the bloke who used to own the garage. 'Is Don Skipford your father?' Her mum had taken her car to Skipford Garage for as long as she could remember.

'He was. He passed away a few years back.'

'Oh, I'm sorry.'

He shrugged. 'Got a baby on the way, I see.'

It was hard not to notice. Her bump had expanded faster than the universe after the big bang, in the last couple of weeks. 'Yep.'

'Julie, she's my missus, says it's your first.'

'That's right.'

He looked as though he was about to say some more, but Cynthia jumped in, anxious to end the interrogation. 'A full service today, please. When can I pick it up?'

'Four-ish?'

'Great. Thanks.'

As she sauntered along the high street, one of her mum's friends recognised her. 'Cynthia Smart, is that you?'

'Mrs Brown? How are you?'

'Not so bad, apart from this darned arthritis. Your mum said you were home for a while. She also said you were in the family way. Got long to go?'

'Eight weeks.'

'Not long. But long enough,' she added with a sympathetic chuckle. 'She said you might be moving back for good.'

Cynthia gave a vague smile. 'Possibly. Not sure yet. There's lots to sort out. Nice to see you again, Mrs Brown.'

'You too, Cynthia. I remember when you were little—'

'I've got to run, sorry. Mum wants me to take her some flour; she's baking a cake for the Harvest Festival. Maybe another time?'

'We can't hold up her baking, now, can we? You take care of yourself and that little one.' To Cynthia's consternation, the elderly woman patted her gently on the tummy.

Cynthia hurried away, recalling it was this very intrusiveness and nosiness that had made her want to leave Little Milling when she was a teenager. That and the total lack of anything exciting to do.

Not wanting to return to the cottage just yet, she decided to treat herself. The bakery had a café attached to it and over tea and cake, and more smiled hellos as villagers recognised her, Cynthia came to the conclusion the village nosiness wasn't such a bad thing. There was a definite sense of community and of people looking out for one another, and it was a pleasant contrast to her friendless life in London, and a stark reminder of how lonely and soulless the city could be.

She decided to take a slice of lemon drizzle back for her mum. Even though Maggie was a keen baker, she might enjoy something she didn't have to make herself.

Her mother insisted on putting the kettle on the second Cynthia arrived home. 'Aren't you having some?'

'I ate mine in the coffee shop. It would be greedy to have another.'

'Nonsense. You're eating for two.'

'You can say that again,' Cynthia muttered. It was more like she was eating for six. S

he recognised it for what it was – comfort eating – and she felt a degree of affinity for those heroines in the movies who

211

reached for a bucket of Ben and Jerry's ice cream when they got dumped. No wonder she was expanding so fast. Unfortunately, it wasn't just the baby who was growing. She was going to have a devil of a job shifting those excess pounds later.

Sod it; who cares, she thought, and reached for the biscuit tin. A cup of tea needed a biscuit to go with it, and she picked out three.

They took their drinks outside, Cynthia determined to enjoy the last of the fine weather, and had just settled down to enjoy their elevenses, when there was the rumble of an engine in the lane. A second or so later, they heard a knock at the door.

Cynthia picked up her cup. She loved that her mum insisted on proper cups and saucers made out of bone china. It seemed to make the act of making and drinking tea a more pleasurable experience than simply dunking a teabag in a mug and swilling it around for a bit. The pattern was pretty, too.

'Are you expecting a delivery?' she asked her mother, who shook her head. Cynthia got to her feet.

'You stay there. I'll go,' Maggie insisted. 'I'm not too old that I can't answer my own front door.'

'I didn't say you were. I need the exercise, that's all.'

Her mum reached up to stroke Cynthia's cheek. 'You're beautiful just the way you are.'

'You have to say that; you're my mum. It's a legal requirement, or something.'

The knock came again.

'I'd better answer it,' Cynthia said, 'before whoever it is gets fed up and goes away, then we'll spend the rest of the day wondering who it could have been.'

She didn't know what made her peep through the living room window before she went into the hall, but when Cynthia saw who it was, she was mighty glad she checked first.

It was Max.

Her breath whooshed out of her and she put a hand to her heart, as she eased away from the window, praying he wouldn't notice the movement.

He was half turned away, and all she could see was his profile, but she drank the sight of him in, her heart thumping madly and her mouth suddenly dry.

Her first thought was, "what was he doing here?" quickly followed by "hadn't he caused enough damage"?

Galvanised into action by a third, louder knock, she darted through the living room, back into the kitchen, and out into the garden.

'Mum! It's Max. You have to get rid of him. Don't let on that I'm here. If he asks, tell him you've no idea where I am.' Thank goodness her car was in the garage, else it would have been a dead giveaway if it had been parked in the lane where it had resided for the past two weeks.

Maggie got to her feet. 'What's going on?'

'I'll tell you later.' She gave her mum a little push towards the kitchen door. 'Hurry, before he decides to come around the back. I'll be in the shed.'

'The *shed?*'

'Yes. Please, mum, get rid of him. For me?' She didn't honestly think he'd come around the back and poke his head into the garden, but she wasn't taking any chances.

Maggie huffed, but she did as she was asked and trotted inside.

Cynthia made a dash for the shed. Then shot back to the

213

patio, grabbed her cup and saucer just in case he did take it upon himself to wander down the side of the cottage – two cups and saucers would be a dead giveaway – and yanked open the shed door.

It was a bit of a tight fit, what with all the gardening paraphernalia that was in there, and she had to make a conscious effort not to squeal when something brushed against the top of her head, but she managed it.

With bated breath and trembling fingers (so much so that the cup rattled in the saucer and she had to put it down on a shelf), Cynthia strained to listen.

Nothing.

All she could hear was a blackbird singing away in the hedge and the coo of a pigeon on the roof.

It seemed like an age before her mum finally came back into the garden, Max-less thankfully, and called to her. 'You can come out now.'

Cynthia breathed a sigh of relief and eased the shed door open, frantically brushing at her clothes as she emerged. 'Cobwebs, yuck,' she said.

Her mum wasn't going to be deflected by talk of cobwebs. Or any other topic, for that matter. Cynthia recognised the set of her mouth and the steely glint in her eye.

'Right, my darling girl, I think you owe me an explanation.'

'It's complicated.'

'I'm not a Facebook page.'

Cynthia glanced at her mum in surprise.

'I do know what social media is,' Maggie responded tartly. 'Spill.'

'I just don't want to have any contact with anyone from work at the moment,' she began.

Her mother folded her arms and raised her eyebrows.

Cynthia sighed.

'Try again,' Maggie said, 'and this time less fibbing and more truth telling. I know when you're lying, Cynthia.'

'The job at Greenleaves has fallen through.'

'How? Why?' She put a hand to her mouth.

'Max lied to me.'

'About the job?' Her mum was incredulous.

'No, at least, I don't think so.'

'Is he married?' She stared shrewdly at her. She had guessed there was more to the colleague relationship than Cynthia was admitting to.

'No!'

'What is it, then? He thinks the world of you, anyone can see that.'

'He's Ricky Webber's son.'

'So?'

'Ricky, my boss? The CEO of the Webber Corporation?' When her mum failed to say anything, Cynthia cried, 'Don't you get it? Ricky brought him in to take over the business.'

'So?' her mother repeated.

'That job should be mine. I worked for it, I earned it.'

'Blood is thicker than water,' Maggie said. 'You can't expect Ricky to choose you over his own son.'

Cynthia frowned and gazed at a bush. It had loads of pretty flowers and the bees were making themselves busy gathering the nectar.

'Don't sulk, it's not nice.' Maggie began eating her cake, and Cynthia shot her a venomous look. How could she eat at a time like this?

'The job should be mine,' she repeated stubbornly.

'I thought you didn't want it,' her mum pointed out. 'Else why would you consider the job with Max. He's looking a bit haggard, by the way. Is that anything to do with you?'

Haggard? Him? 'I doubt it.'

'Does it matter if he didn't tell you he was Ricky's son? From what you've told me about your boss, I'm pretty sure I wouldn't want to admit to being related to that man, either.'

'He knew I wanted the CEO job. He knew! Yet, he didn't tell me it was his for the taking.'

'Does he want it?' her mum asked, reasonably.

'He says not.'

'There you go, then.'

'It's still not acceptable, Mum. How can I trust him after this? What did he want anyway?' she asked, somewhat belatedly.

'He wanted to know if you were here.'

'Did he say why?'

Her mother huffed. 'No, but I must say, I didn't feel comfortable lying to him.'

'What did you say, exactly?'

'Do you care? He's gone; isn't that what you wanted?'

'Yes. No. Bugger.'

'You need to sort out what it is you *do* want.'

'I know. But he lied to me.'

'So did you, or rather, you made me do it for you. And telling a fib isn't a good enough reason to refuse a job offer. Or to refuse him.'

Cynthia wasn't sure it was either, but how could she trust him after this? Especially when she didn't want her heart to be broken any worse than it was already.

216

Chapter 32

Three and a half weeks was long enough to spend at her mum's house. Cynthia supposed that out of the whole sorry mess, she did have one thing to thank Max for – the realisation she couldn't live with her mother for any length of time.

Being in her mum's house was like being fifteen all over again. She'd found herself pulling faces at the back of her mum's head when she'd been told off for leaving a plate on the coffee table and not immediately washing it up. Then there was the exaggerated worry her mum had that Cynthia had left her straighteners on. She'd only ever done that once. Once! And that was when she'd come home from university in her second year. The way her mother was acting, it was as if it was a common occurrence. It had happened twenty-five years ago, for God's sake. There was no need for her mum to mention it. Every. Single. Day.

It was time she went back to London, back to her own space, back to work, and back to the life she was trying so hard to pretend didn't exist.

The fact that she now knew that living with her mum wouldn't work, offered her some small amount of consolation for telling Max where to stick his job.

That she had to resume her old life in the city, counter-balanced said consolation.

What she wanted, in an ideal world, was to live in the same village as her mum (or maybe the next one over…?), to have a job that paid the bills yet didn't demand her soul in exchange, and to be able to raise her child where she could play outdoors and not be choked by exhaust fumes.

Was it too much to ask?

Probably, because just when it had been within her grasp, it had been cruelly snatched away from her. And that was without bringing her feelings for Max into the equation.

Max… she wished her wayward thoughts would stop turning to him. Maybe when she was back at work, she'd be too busy to think about him.

It would probably be wishful thinking, because he would still be in the building, cosying up to his father and jamming his foot firmly in the Webber Corporation's door.

The mere thought gave her palpitations, but no matter how she felt about him she had to return to work. For one thing, her doctor's note only had another few days left to run, and for another, if it was extended any further Ricky would be well within his rights to begin her maternity leave before she was ready, and that was something she wanted to avoid at all costs. The more time she had off on maternity leave prior to the baby being born, then the less time she'd be able to have off after her daughter was here. Although Cynthia still didn't know the sex of her baby, she was continuing to run with her gut instinct and the vision she'd had of a dark haired little girl in a bath full of bubbles that she'd had the evening she'd discovered she was pregnant. And she was determined to spend as much time with her little daughter as she possibly could before she was forced to return to the daily grind.

Cynthia wasn't certain, but she had a feeling her mother had been relieved when Cynthia had told her she was going back to London, although the alacrity with which she'd helped her pack yesterday evening was a bit of a clue.

All that was needed this morning was to shower, dress, have breakfast and say goodbye.

'I'll miss you,' Maggie declared, enveloping her in a massive hug, at the same time careful not to squash her bump. 'I've loved having you here.'

Cynthia pulled back a little and grinned. 'For the first couple of days, maybe.'

Maggie made a face. 'I must admit, I have become very used to my own company over the years.'

'I know; you have your way of doing things and I have mine, and I think we're both too independent to live together.'

'It would be nice if you were closer, though.'

Cynthia had to agree.

That thought was on her mind most of the way back, but the closer she got to London, then the more her thoughts switched to her rather impressive to-do list. First on it was to arrange an appointment with a nursery or two. Now that she had some idea of how long she was going to be on maternity leave for, she could give the nursery a date for when she'd need to start.

She was still mulling things over when she opened the door to her apartment and almost tripped over a long slim box lying in the hall.

Flowers, sent by Sally, and now long dead.

Tears pricked at the back of her eyes. Apart from a pile of flyers and several letters which were of no importance, it appeared no one had noticed or cared she was on sick leave. Except for Sally. It occurred to her that Ricky hadn't bothered to contact her at all. Not a call, or a text, or even an email. Nothing.

How sad was that?

She'd worked at the Webber Corporation for nearly all her adult life, and she'd known Ricky for almost as long. Yet he hadn't even dropped her an email to see how she was.

Neither had anyone else. She didn't have friends – only those people she met in work, or because of work. Not even Sally was a friend, because how can you have a genuine friendship with someone you might need to discipline one day?

Still, it was very nice of her to send the flowers, and Cynthia made a mental note to give her a call and let her know when she'd be back in the office.

For now, though, she'd better get her backside into gear, because she'd not bought anything much for the baby, apart from those few things all those weeks ago. And she couldn't for the life of her remember where she'd put them.

She intended to use the rest of the week wisely to prepare for her baby's arrival, and with that in mind she opened a couple of windows to air the apartment out, made a hot drink, and switched her computer on.

For a half an hour, she was focused and determined, but after checking out over ten nurseries, and making appointments to visit three of them, she began to flag, and ended up on what had quickly become one of her favourite sites.

Her baby was about the size of a pineapple, she read, thinking the child was as spiky as one as a foot jabbed her in the stomach. It was most definitely a foot, and she marvelled as she felt the shape of it through her skin.

'Not long now, little one,' she crooned. 'It's about time I bought you some clothes. And a cot. And—'

Ooh, look, the baby's fingernails should be quite long now. Not manicure long, but they should be reaching the ends of her fingertips, and she should open her eyes when she was awake and keep them closed when she was asleep. What could her little girl see in there in the dark warmth of her womb?

Apparently, her little one should weigh five and a half pounds and she could be as much as eighteen inches long. No wonder Cynthia felt like she was carrying a baby elephant.

She looked up from her screen and gave a gentle stretch. She found she became stiff quite quickly if she remained in one position for too long, but walking around was too much of an effort. So, a careful stretch would have to do.

The baby moved again, and this time Cynthia thought it might be an elbow or a knee which was poking out this time. She stroked her bulge sorrowfully – how nice would it be to share this precious moment with someone. A sudden longing for her mother overtook her, and she sniffed loudly. Even bloody Max sodding Oakland would be better than no one…

Crossly, she turned her attention back to the screen, this time to concentrate on the hunt for a cot and a pram. She felt as though she should buy these large pieces of equipment in person, but she honestly didn't feel like traipsing around the shops on her own. It was simply too depressing and too tiring.

Confused at the sheer amount of stuff out there, she clicked on one item after another. There was so much choice, she didn't know where to start. She did manage to buy a cot and arrange for it to be delivered, but she wasn't sure it was the best one or the right one for her and the baby. She would have loved to ask someone she knew for advice; it was a pity Lara was part of the Max package, because Cynthia felt the pair of them had clicked. The woman also had young children, so would know what was what.

Feeling more alone than she had ever been in her life, totally confused, apprehensive, and rather scared of what the future might hold, Cynthia let her tears fall.

No one said this was going to be easy. In fact, she'd been repeatedly warned it wouldn't be. But she was healthy and so was her baby, she had a roof over her head and money in the bank – so why did she feel so bloody scared and broken hearted?

Damn Max. Damn him to hell.

Chapter 33

'It's lovely to see you!' Sally exclaimed, bending down to give Cynthia a kiss on the cheek when she made to get up. Her PA slid into the seat opposite and scrutinised her.

Luigi's was packed, and Cynthia had arrived a little early to bag a table. They could have met somewhere else, but the food here was good and it was near the office, so Sally wouldn't have to spend half of her lunchbreak travelling across town. The fact that this was where Cynthia and Max usually came for lunch, had absolutely no bearing on things. None whatsoever.

'Do I pass muster?' Cynthia asked, sardonically, as Sally gave her a thorough going over.

'What is muster?' Sally wanted to know.

'No idea.'

'Whatever it is, you pass it. You're positively blooming.'

'You can say that again. Although "blooming" isn't the word that springs to mind.'

'Seriously, you look great; a little tired maybe, but I

223

remember how difficult it is to sleep well when you've a growing baby in your tummy. How far are you now?'

'Thirty-four weeks. I'm officially eight months pregnant.'

'You said you're coming back to work? Are you sure?' A waitress appeared at Sally's elbow. 'Should we order first, then we can catch up properly?'

'Always the PA,' Cynthia laughed. 'Always organising things.'

They perused the menu for a moment, then gave their orders. As soon as the server left, Sally asked, 'How are you feeling? Honestly feeling, I mean; not your usual "I'm fine" standard reply.'

Cynthia grimaced. 'You know me too well. Thanks for the flowers, by the way. They were beautiful, and so thoughtful.'

'I dithered about sending them because I thought you might have loads, but then I thought, what the hell, you can never have too many bouquets, right?'

Little did her PA know that they had been the only flowers she'd received, and they were long dead by the time Cynthia unpacked them. She suspected they had been gorgeous once, though.

'Don't think I didn't notice you haven't answered my question,' Sally observed, picking up a jug of water that had just been placed on the table and pouring them both a glass.

'You're right, I am tired. All the blimmin' time. And I'm eating like a horse. My blood pressure is only slightly raised now, so the fears of pre-eclampsia were unfounded. I'm glad the doctor signed me off work, though. It was fantastic spending time with my mum, but I'm ready to return to work.' She took a sip of her drink, her mouth dry. 'Any gossip?' she asked, lightly.

Sally said, 'Mr Webber seconded me to his office now Angela has left, and he's only gone and dumped a big party in my lap. He's trying to schmooze some American company, and considering Halloween is such a huge deal over there, he thought it would be a great idea to hold a Halloween party for them. He seems to think I can magic it all out of thin air. It's only two weeks away now and I'm up to my eyeballs in smoke machines and spider webs.'

'Will I get you back, do you think?'

'Oh, yes. His new PA starts on Monday, but I expect she'll need her hand holding for a bit, until she settles in. In one way, it's worked out quite well, because you're only going to be back for a couple of weeks anyway, aren't you, so I can work with her until you come back off maternity leave.'

'I'm not going on maternity leave for another six weeks. I'm not starting it until I absolutely have to.'

'Oh?' Sally's eyes widened and she raised her eyebrows. 'Please don't leave it too late. I don't want to be delivering your baby in the office,' she joked. 'You'll make a mess of the carpet tiles.'

'God forbid! I hope that doesn't happen; I fancy soft music and candles, and lots of pain relief.' Cynthia hadn't actually chosen anything – all she knew was that she was having her baby in hospital with as much pain relief as she could persuade the midwives and doctors to give her. Now she came to think of it though, candles and soft music did sound nice.

'Are you going to be all right coming back?' Sally asked. 'I feel dreadful about it all.'

'About telling me Max is Ricky's son?'

Sally nodded. 'If I hadn't said anything, then you wouldn't have confronted him and—'

'There's no harm done. The baby and I are fine. And you had to tell me – imagine if I'd found out after…' Cynthia trailed off. She'd not shared Max's offer of a job with her PA, and neither had she shared the details of her burgeoning love for him with her. 'I'll be OK. I'm sure I can manage to avoid him for six weeks.' She didn't mention how she would cope after her maternity leave, because she didn't know whether she'd be returning to the Webber Corporation or not; it all depended on how the job hunting went.

'He's left,' Sally said.

'Pardon?'

'Max has gone. I don't know the details, but the day after you went to the hospital, he cleared his desk and he hasn't been seen since. Molly in HR says his details have been archived, and he's no longer on the payroll.'

Cynthia was frozen. It was all well and good her saying she never wanted to see him again and that she was sure she could avoid him until the end of November, but that had been on her terms. Now he'd left though, the decision had been taken out of her hands, and she had a feeling he wouldn't go looking for her or try to contact her again.

The knowledge made her want to cry.

Her distress must have shown in her face, because Sally was apologising all over again, and blaming herself for Cynthia's mad dash to the hospital and subsequent flight to Little Milling.

'I feel so guilty,' her PA was saying.

'Don't be. You did me a favour, plus I love being off work.' That was only partly true. Since she'd been back in London, she hated it. The days had dragged, despite her cramming them full of shopping and planning for the baby. The nights had been twice as long. While she was at her mum's she'd not felt quite as bad, and at least she'd had company. But she hadn't been able to settle there either, and now she was back in the city and surrounded by all those millions of people, her loneliness was so acute it hurt.

If she was honest, she missed Max. She missed their weekly lunches, their banter, his smile. His kiss.

Why, oh why, did he have to go and spoil it all?

Abruptly, her eyes filled with tears and they spilt over to trickle down her cheeks. She was turning into a right old cry baby lately, and she hated herself for being so weak and emotional all the time.

'It's the hormones,' she explained, dabbing at her face with a napkin.

'It's not,' Sally countered, knowingly. 'There's more going on with you than mere hormones. If you tell me about it, I might be able to help.'

So Cynthia did. She told Sally everything and it felt good to talk about it. But even as she was regaling her PA with every miserable detail of her disastrous love life and equally disastrous job offer, she knew deep down no one and nothing would help her recover from a broken heart.

Chapter 34

Cynthia's hands shook. It was barely noticeable (she hoped) but she was aware of it and her nerves irritated her beyond measure. If she could have avoided returning to the Webber Corporation, she would have done. But six weeks maternity leave at 90 per cent pay was not to be sneezed at.

Suddenly six weeks didn't seem nearly long enough to spend with a newborn, but she hadn't any choice. How the hell she thought she could return to work two weeks after giving birth, was beyond her.

She slipped into her office unnoticed. Not many staff were in at six-thirty in the morning, although Ricky undoubtedly would be. His office was on the floor above though, so the chances of accidentally bumping into him were slim, thankfully, and she was fairly sure he wouldn't venture down onto the directors' floor to seek her out. If he was even aware she was back.

It was strange not to see Sally's umbrella in the coat stand, or the photo of her and her husband on her desk, and Cynthia knew she was going to miss her.

It was sensible though, for her to show Ricky's new PA the ropes, and Sally would only be twiddling her thumbs while Cynthia was off. She'd be lost without her though, even if she was only tying up loose ends and handing the more urgent stuff over to someone else.

She switched on her laptop and waited for it to load. The loose ends bit wasn't going to take long, so she'd scheduled an early finish to check out the nurseries. She was pretty certain no one would miss her, and no one would care.

Considering she'd been a big fish in this tepid pond (if she was going to stick with aquatic analogies, Ricky was the shark, she was the considerably smaller shark), she was now reduced to being a skate or a plaice – no one noticed her in the sand in the bottom and she might as well be invisible. Without Sally to keep her company, she was lonelier than ever, and she marvelled at how far and how fast she'd fallen in such a short space of time.

Somehow, she muddled through the day, until finally the time came when she was able to shrug on her coat (it was the middle of October now and the temperature was dropping) and disappear out of the building. No one said a word to her on the way out, apart from the security guy, Ian.

He gave her a wave and mouthed 'Nice to see you back,' at her.

He hadn't been on duty this morning – it had been someone new, who hadn't recognised her and who'd scrutinised her ID for so long and so thoroughly she felt quite guilty – and it brought it home to her how easily she had been replaced and forgotten. Now that she wasn't working on anything important, it was as though she didn't exist.

Little Leapers looked good on paper, even if she'd had to do a double-take when she'd initially seen their logo as she thought it had read Lepers, not Leapers. Unfortunately, the nursery didn't look as good in real life. She didn't know what it was, but there was something about it she didn't like and no matter how hard she tried, she couldn't put her finger on it. It appeared to tick all the boxes, and the staff were engaged with the children in various activities. The children themselves seemed contented enough and the facilities were top-notch (so they should be for the prices they were charging), but.... nah. This one wasn't for her.

Next, she tried *Baby Birds*, which had two sections, Hatchlings for the very little ones, and Fledgelings for those who could toddle about on their own. Once again, it was perfectly acceptable, but it was only when she looked around it and moved onto and discarded the third, *Acorns*, did she understand there was nothing wrong with any of the nurseries per se. It was Cynthia herself who was the problem; she simply didn't want to leave her baby in any of them.

With a deep sigh, she turned around and went back inside *Acorns*. At least it was the closest to her apartment and had the shortest number of letters to type into her online diary. And without any better reason to choose this one rather than either of the others, she signed on the dotted line. With her baby duly enrolled, she gave the place a final glance, and realised this was going to be her child's home for most of the day five days a week. It made her feel incredibly sad.

There was something she could do to cheer herself up however, and that was to go shopping. The baby needed stuff

– lots of stuff, and she'd start with bedding for the cot which was due to be delivered later today. She'd just have time to pop into the baby shop on her way home, and see what they had.

Oh, my word, she thought, gazing around in delight. Everything was painted in a delicate shade of mint and there were separate sections for tiny babies and for older ones, and they were all colour coordinated. Naturally, she gravitated towards the tiniest of clothes, stroking their delicately soft fabrics and marvelling at just how wee some of the things were.

'When are you due?' one of the assistants asked and Cynthia turned to her with a smile.

She knew asking her that particular question was a sales technique, but she didn't care. It was nice to be asked, and she took the opportunity to pick the girl's brains regarding cot bedding.

Unsurprisingly, she emerged with several carrier bags bulging with everything she could possibly need for a new baby to have the perfect night's sleep, and she made her way home feeling quite pleased that at least she'd managed to achieve something today.

She'd left a key with the man who was decorating the nursery, and she was happy to see he was making good progress. He'd finished for the day but the smell of fresh paint lingered and she opened a window to dispel it. The second coat of the most delicious shade of pale lemon had gone on the walls, and he only had to fit a new blind for her and rehang the door, and he was done.

She'd just put her bags in the living room, when her doorbell rang, and for a moment she had a wild hope it was Max. Then reality kicked in and she remembered about the cot.

'Can you put it in there?' she asked, directing the delivery men into the newly decorated nursery. They obliged and even unpacked it for her, taking the large box and assorted packaging materials away with them.

Of course, now it had arrived, Cynthia simply had to put it together. All those cute soft sheets and blankets were crying out to be put on it, so she microwaved a ready meal, ate some fruit, and then set to.

It was only like Lego or Meccano, she told herself, checking she had the right pieces and reading the instructions carefully. How hard can it be?

An hour and a half later, she finally admitted defeat. It was a two-person job, and the baby inside her didn't count. Every time she tried to marry up one side with another, the side she'd already put together but not tightened up (because the instructions said not to) fell apart.

Feeling utterly useless and quite sorry for herself, Cynthia slid down the newly painted wall and sat on the floor in a heap. But she was determined she wasn't going to cry. She'd done so much of that over the past month that she felt pretty cross with herself. She was stronger than this. She was a capable, resourceful woman, and if she couldn't put this sodding thing together on her own, then she'd get a man in to do it for her.

Max's face popped into her head and she batted it away.

Now wasn't a good time to be thinking of him. There never *was* a good time to think of him. All it did was make her heart ache more than it did already.

So why did she clamber ungainly to her feet and waddle over to the computer? And why did she then type his name into a search engine? These past four weeks, she'd managed to block him from her life completely. No calls, no messages, certainly no face to face meetings (although she had to admit it had been a close call in Little Milling). She had been resolute in her determination not to look him up on social media, and neither had she Googled Greenleaves. Apart from him sabotaging her thoughts every so often, which she couldn't do anything about, she'd succeeded in pretending he didn't exist.

Which was why she failed to understand her stupid impulse.

Now she'd typed his name in, she couldn't not look, could she? Besides, she desperately wanted to see his face one more time. Was that too much to ask?

There he was, handsome and incredibly sexy, and she traced her forefinger down his cheek, noting the lack of lines around his eyes. His hair was as dark as she remembered it, although she could have sworn there were a few silver strands in real life which weren't in the photo.

Clicking on the link, she saw it was an article in a local paper on how he'd set up the hotel and the farm (she hadn't realised he owned that too – something else he had failed to share with her, although this piece of information was none of her business) and it was over ten years old. There was no mention of his connection to Ricky Webber, although she had no idea why there should be. Ricky was wealthy but he was hardly of the same ilk as Richard Branson.

As she gazed at Max's image, Cynthia wondered how she was going to live without seeing him again. Incredibly, after the way he had deceived her, she missed him so much it was a physical ache.

Don't be silly, she told herself. A couple of kisses did not a relationship make, and that was all that had taken place between them. So what exactly was she grieving for? The loss of a job which meant she could escape the rat race in London? The loss of a future which had him in it? The loss of her heart

– because there was no denying the fact that she'd given it to him. It had been a slow process, and she hadn't been entirely aware it was happening until it was a fait accompli, but there was no going back.

Had he cared for her at all, or had it been a complete sham, a design to deflect her focus away from the chief executive job? If it was the latter, he'd succeeded.

But – and this was something she was having trouble reconciling with his betrayal – he had walked away from the Webber Corporation, his fast-track promotion, and his father.

Had he been telling the truth about not being interested?

Whatever; it was too late now. She'd made her bed and she'd have to damned well lie in it, no matter how much it hurt.

Chapter 35

Could she get any bigger? Cynthia had an awful suspicion that with four weeks still to go and her baby reported to be gaining half a pound a week from now until the birth, she was going to be ginormous by the time she went into labour. She could barely reach the keyboard on her desk; her arms were hardly long enough to reach because her bump was in the way.

This last week had been a bit of a drag, if she was honest, and she was becoming seriously fed up with being pregnant. It wasn't fun anymore and the excitement had worn off to be replaced with impatience and a growing dread of what was to come.

Aside from the very real fear of the birth itself, she was faced with a steadily increasing worry about how she was going to cope. Everything she read (and she read *a lot*) only reinforced her concern that she was going to struggle on her own. What if things went wrong and she had to have a Caesarean? There was no way she'd manage to look after a tiny baby whilst recovering from what was essentially quite a major operation.

She should go to her mum's house and have the baby in St Richards Hospital in Chichester. That would be the sensible thing to do, and the more she thought about it the better the idea sounded. Her mum would be delighted to have her in the short term (long term was a different kettle of fish) and she could certainly do with another pair of hands and some maternal fussing and looking after.

It would be a nuisance to change hospitals and midwives at this late stage, but it was for the best.

Making a note in her online diary for tomorrow to start the ball rolling – after she'd spoken to her mum of course, which she planned on doing when she got back to her apartment later – she was about to double-check a contract she'd been working on, when Sally sashayed into her office and stuffed a carrier bag under her desk. It was Halloween and the party kicked off in less than an hour.

'You look nice,' Cynthia said. Sally did a twirl. 'I never thought a female version of Frankenstein's monster could look so effective.'

'By rights, I suppose I should have gone as Bride of Frankenstein, but I was too mean to shell out for the costume when my other half had an old suit that would fit. I had to alter it, but I think it works.'

It did. Sally had tailored the jacket so it nipped in at the waist and gave her some definition, and her make-up was expertly applied. She dropped into her chair, took a compact mirror out of her bag, and checked her heavy eye-liner, then turned her face from side to side and patted at the greenish tinge on her forehead.

'How did you get the bolt to stick on your neck?' Cynthia wanted to know.

'Wires, see?' She turned around to show her.

'Clever.'

'Are you sure you don't want to come?'

'I could go as the incredible expanding woman,' Cynthia joked. 'Seriously, I'm not in the mood for a party. Not only that but I don't have a costume, I can't drink, everything I eat gives me heartburn, my boobs are leaking, and no one, least of all Ricky, wants to chat about piles or Braxton Hicks.'

Sally laughed. 'Fair point, but you could go as a beach ball. Petra from Accounts is a dab hand with the face paints. If you ask her, she'll happily draw one on your stomach. Hang on…' Sally narrowed her eyes. 'Why are you still here? You should have gone home an hour ago.'

'I want to finish checking over a contract while I've got the energy. I seem to be on a roll lately – last night I scrubbed the bathroom from ceiling to floor, and I had a mad urge to clean the oven this morning. I didn't act on it, though; I had a cup of tea instead and waited for it to pass,' she joked.

Sally smiled.

There was a brief silence, then her PA said, 'Um, have you been in contact with Max?'

Cynthia gave Sally a sharp look. 'No. Why would I have?'

'I wondered, that's all.'

'Have you heard anything I need to know about?'

Her PA shook her head. 'Nothing. Are you sure he hasn't—?' She stopped and bit her lip.

'You'd better get going,' Cynthia said, 'and leave me in peace. The sooner I get this contract looked at, the sooner I will go home.'

Sally took the hint that Cynthia didn't want to discuss Max. She didn't want to think about him because it upset her. Why Sally felt the need to bring his name into the conversation, she didn't know.

'Don't work too hard, will you?' her PA said, waggling her fingers at her as she retreated to the door.

'I won't, I promise; now skedaddle.'

Cynthia waited for the outer door to close and then she sat back with a heavy sigh. Going to a party like this one would have been the highlight of her week once upon a time. All that networking and connection-making would have seen her as happy as a dog with two tails. Now though, the idea was abhorrent to her. She couldn't think of anything she'd like to do less.

Oh, how her life had changed in the five months since she discovered she was pregnant. She couldn't imagine dressing up to go to a party, and especially not a fancy dress one (she wouldn't find anything to fit anyway). Her ankles were swollen, everything ached (her back was the worst) and all she would be able to manage on the dancing front would be a duck-like waddle. To top it all off, her pelvis hurt this evening, and the baby felt heavy and incredibly low, dragging her down.

She should go home now, but the contract carried a deadline of tomorrow at five p.m. and she didn't want to leave it until then in case there were any nasty surprises. It might as well be done now, and if there were any issues with it she could deal with them in the morning.

Cynthia was knee deep in formal language and her eyes were starting to blur, when her phone buzzed. Glad for the distraction, she picked it up. Sally, bless her, was checking up on her and she smiled when she read the text asking her if she was still in the office. She debated whether to fib and say she had left and was on her way home. However, she wouldn't put it past her PA to check with Ian on security in the morning, so she texted back that she was still here, finishing up by promising she would go home in a few minutes. She fully intended to, because even the cleaning staff had come and gone and there was no one left on her floor, possibly not in the rest of the building.

Now that she thought about it, it was a bit eerie here on her own. There hadn't been another soul on her floor since Sally had gone (everyone was no doubt at the party), and even the cleaners had come and gone. Ian would still be in the foyer, and she felt guilty because the poor security guard would be unable to lock up and go home until everyone had left the building, and she had a feeling she was the last one here. It wasn't fair of her to keep him there, but as she switched the office lights off and closed the lid of her laptop, she decided he'd have to wait a few more minutes because she'd better go to the loo before she began her journey home.

While she was washing her hands, her phone rang.

It was Sally again.

'I just texted you. You can stop nagging – I'm just about to leave,' Cynthia said, a warm feeling spreading through her chest at the thought that someone else besides her mother cared.

'I'm glad I caught you,' Sally cried, and Cynthia heard the anxiety in her voice. 'I've lost my necklace; you know, the one I always wear. I think it might have been when I was getting changed, although I can remember having it when I was in your office, because I sat at my desk to apply some more green stuff before I left and I can remember tucking it inside my T-

239

shirt. You wouldn't be a love and have a quick look for it?'

The warm feeling dissipated. 'Of course I will. I'll let you know either way, so give me a few minutes.'

Sally said, 'Don't worry if you can't find it, just have a quick look. It might have dropped in a drawer or fallen in the bag of works clothes I stuffed under my desk.' She sounded quite anxious, despite what she said, and Cynthia knew how much she valued the necklace.

She made her way slowly back to her office, wincing as she walked. The baby was weighing extremely heavy this evening, and she had the dragging sensation low down in her tummy that she used to associate with the imminent arrival of her period. Her back was in bits, and she was looking forward to a hot bath to ease the aches and pains when she got home. A glass of wine would have been nice too, but she'd have to settle for a cup of cocoa.

She struggled down the corridor, her hands massaging the small of her back, and waddled into the outer office where Sally had her desk. The surface was clear, apart from a monitor, a mouse, and a keyboard, which she lifted up to check underneath, already knowing it was unlikely the necklace would be hiding there.

Wincing, she got slowly and clumsily down on her knees to peer under the desk – gone were the days where she'd simply be able to bend at the waist, and she had a disconcerting thought she might never be able to bend like that again.

Feeling around in the gloom and wishing she'd had the foresight to switch the lights back on, she thought she imagined the noise at first.

Then she heard it again. Soft footsteps in the corridor outside.

Her blood turned to ice, her heart began to flutter, and a cold prickle of dread trickled down her neck as she realised there wasn't anyone left in the building apart from her and whoever was moving around outside the office. Who on earth could—?

She realised immediately who it must be, and she took a deep breath, rolling her eyes at her stupidity. It was only Ian, come to winkle her out of her office and insist she went home, which she would do once she'd checked in the carrier bag Sally had stashed under her desk.

'Ian?' she called. 'Give me a second and I'll be out of your hair and on my way.'

No answer.

Frowning, because she could have sworn he was definitely just outside the door, she awkwardly backed out of the small space and heaved herself to her feet, using the desk for support, and grunting with the effort.

Her back seriously ached now and her stomach felt uncomfortably tight, as though there was a band around it giving it a squeeze. Those Braxton Hicks were getting stronger, and they were becoming quite painful now.

Leaning heavily on the desk to catch her breath, she swivelled around.

Her waters broke at the exact same time she saw who was standing in the doorway.

Chapter 36

Cynthia stood, horrified, as liquid gushed down her legs and puddled on the carpet. Eyes wide, she stared at the liquid, then she slowly raised her head to look at Max.

He was frozen, his own gaze on the wet patch beneath her feet.

Cynthia clutched her stomach with her one hand; the other still grasped the desk, keeping her upright. She had an awful feeling she might be about to keel over.

Panic beat at her mind with flapping wings, dark and frantic.

His eyes came up to meet hers and she saw her own fear reflected in his face. It was only there a moment, then it was gone. That it had been there at all, almost stopped her heart.

He took a step towards her.

Her sudden gasp of pain brought him to a halt.

She had an image of his face, shocked and white, before her mind turned inward and all she was aware of was the savage pain ripping through her, squeezing her innards until she felt sure the baby would burst through her skin, tearing her apart from the inside out.

Dear God, she'd never known such white-hot agony, and it knocked her senseless, leaving her panting and breathless as she bent over the desk, trying not to scream.

She felt his hands on her back, rubbing, soothing, his voice in her ear. She had no idea what he was saying – the only voice she understood was the one in her head repeating over and over again that the baby was too early, it was too soon.

Gradually, the awful crushing pain dimmed and she could breathe again, the breaths short and panting, and her racing heart slowed enough for her to register what he was saying, the thunder in her ears subsiding to a dull roar.

Calmly, he said. 'I'm going to help you downstairs and take you to the hospital.'

'The baby is coming.' Her voice was shaking.

'I know.'

'It's too early.'

'Yes, but not that early. It'll be OK, my love.'

She wanted to believe him, she *had* to believe him. Thirty-six weeks wasn't that early. Babies who were born much earlier survived.

The fear wasn't listening. It scratched at her mind with gnarled fingers, and she shuddered.

Max's arms were around her, holding her up, bearing the weight of her and her baby, preventing her from sinking to the floor.

'Come on, you can do this,' he urged.

'I'm having contractions.'

'Yes, you are, but it was just the one.'

She heard the unspoken "for now", but let him guide her towards the door and into the corridor.

Now that the pain had receded, she became aware her legs were wet and her tights were clinging damply to her skin. Should she take them off?

Maybe she'd do it when she was in the car. The sooner she was heading to the hospital the better.

'This is getting to be a habit,' she said, leaning heavily on him as they made their slow way down the corridor to the lift. 'It's the third time you've had to take me to the hospital.'

Max chuckled, a low rumbling sound. 'Always happy to help.'

She was about to answer when she felt the contraction starting to build. It came from deep within, a steady inexorable pressure, uncomfortable rather than painful at first, then—

Cynthia gasped, her hands on her stomach, low down, supporting the baby as much as she could, its weight solid and unyielding. This new wave was stronger than the first, carrying her with it on its white-tipped surge and her mind went blank as she fought to survive it.

Slowly, slowly, it receded once more, leaving her drained and slick with sweat. 'I think I want to push.'

Max looked horrified. 'You can't. You're probably not dilated enough.'

Panting, she gasped, 'How would you know?'

'Joe. I had the lowdown on Lara each time – in graphic detail. I didn't want to listen, but I guess some of it must have stuck.' He hoisted her bag further onto his shoulder, then put his arm around her waist once more to take some of her weight. 'Can you walk?'

'I'll have to.'

'Lean on me.'

The distance to the lift seemed insurmountable but when she made it without enduring another contraction, she let out a long shuddering breath.

Hang in there, she told the baby silently. Just a little while longer. Please, please don't come out yet.

Max propped her up against the wall and jabbed at the button, tapping his foot impatiently. 'Come on, come on.'

Cynthia heard the distant rumble as the lift trundled into life, and she felt a faint vibration in the wall. How long was it going to take? 'I can't get in a taxi like this.'

'I've got my car. It's parked outside.'

'What are you doing here anyway? Did you come for the party?' He didn't look dressed for Halloween, but then the devil didn't always show his horns and forked tail.

'I came to see you.'

Her legs felt weak and wobbly, and she was desperate to sit down, but there were no chairs in the corridor. 'How did you know I'd still be here? It's late.'

He didn't answer and she tilted her head back to look at him. 'How? she repeated.

It didn't matter and she didn't care, but anything to take her mind off what was happening was welcome and she grasped at it. But the little gibbering voice which played and replayed in her head kept telling her it was too soon, the baby wasn't due yet. It was four weeks early and she wasn't ready. Neither of them were.

Shut up, she wanted to shout at it. She bit her lip instead. Dear God, please let the lift come soon; she had to get to the hospital *now*.

'Was it Sally?' she guessed and his mouth twitched so she knew she was right. 'Just wait until I get my hands—' Cynthia groaned as another pain ripped through her. 'Gah, it hurts,' she cried.

'How long since the last one?

'Stop trying to change the subject,' she snarled through gritted teeth.

'I'm not, this is important. The hospital will want to know. I'd better time them.'

The lift finally arrived and pinged softly open. Max helped her step into it, and she slumped against one corner, breathing heavily. They travelled to the ground floor in silence, both of them watching the numbers count down. Max glanced periodically at his watch.

A slight jolt, another ping and the lift doors opened.

He caught her around the waist again and supported her lurch towards the automatic doors at the far end of the foyer, holding her up. Her legs felt as though they belonged to someone else, and the only real feeling she had came from the crippling band around her stomach which tightened agonisingly again, forcing her to stop and catch her breath before she'd got halfway across the foyer. She could feel her back, too, and the ache in it almost made her cry. But what worried her the most was the intense pressure between her legs.

'I've got to sit down,' she gasped. 'Just for a minute. Oww.' Her wail echoed through the space, bouncing back off the walls and the windows.

Max guided her to the nearest chair and held most of her weight as she lowered herself into it.

When her behind touched the seat, she yelped. 'I can't sit down, it hurts too much. Max, Max!'

'I'm here. Hold your arms out and I'll lift you up. Come on, Cynthia, you can do this. The exit is just over there, and my car is parked right outside.'

'You'll get a ticket.' Was that all she could say? She was about to give birth and the only thing her odd brain was focusing on was Max getting a parking ticket. Dear God…

He half-carried, half-hauled her to the door, and it took every ounce of will power she had not to sink to the floor. She felt an urgent need to be on all fours, an instinctive visceral urge, and she fought to stay upright. She wouldn't get far crawling along the pavement.

'Shit!' Max exclaimed.

'What's wrong?' She ground the question out between gritted teeth, barking the words out.

'The door is locked.'

'Where's Ian?' She tried to straighten up, but she couldn't. Hunched over was the most she could manage.

'No idea.'

'There must be a key somewhere.'

Max began to look worried. 'Stay there. I'll check behind the reception desk.'

Where the hell did he think she was going to go? Roller blading? Nightclubbing? She could hardly walk a step under her own steam, let alone leave the building.

He left her leaning awkwardly against the glass door, and dashed across the foyer to the glossy reception desk, where he began to rifle through it.

'Hurry,' she moaned. She unquestionably did need to push. She wasn't imagining it.

The compulsion was non-negotiable. It was a deep-seated, primal impulse, and her body was going to do it with, or without, her consent.

'I am hurrying,' she heard him say, then her stomach tightened again, catapulting her into grey pain, where the world around her faded for a long moment as the needs of her body claimed her.

When the contraction released her from its grip and she refocused, it was to find Max standing in front of her, his eyes filled with concern. 'I can't find it.'

'Is there a door release button, or something?' she asked, forcing the words out between sharp fast breaths.

'I looked. At least we know Ian is still in the building,' Max said, as if that was any help. She needed the security guard to be here now, right this minute.

'How do you know?' she asked.

'If he'd have left for the night, he would have set the alarms, and most alarm systems these days are triggered by motion. I'll go and find him.'

'Don't you dare leave me. I need Jess. My phone's in my bag. My midwife,' she reminded him, seeing his questioning look.

'Right.'

'*Hurry*! Tell her I'm in labour and on my way in.'

Max found the midwife's number and pressed the call button. 'Is that Jess? I'm with Cynthia Smart. Her waters have broken.'

Cynthia bent over as far as her enormous stomach would allow and groaned. The sound was remarkably similar to the noise the cow had made when she was being milked.

'I'm just about to,' he continued, then, 'I'd say every couple of minutes if I have to guess.' A pause. 'Yes, of course, right away.'

'Well?'

'They're expecting us.'

Cynthia noted the word "us" but didn't comment on it. He was coming with her, and for that she was extremely grateful. Now that the birth was imminent, she had no idea how she thought she'd manage to do this on her own; not when the simple act of getting to the hospital was proving to be such a challenge.

It wasn't supposed to happen like this. She was supposed to have gentle contractions, far apart, which would have allowed her plenty of time to get to the hospital. No way had she anticipated her waters breaking first and this crushing, inexorable agony.

Oh God, she badly wanted to push. But that was ridiculous, wasn't it? Her waters had broken less than fifteen minutes ago – although it did feel much longer – so the baby was nowhere near ready to be born. She had ages to go yet. Though, if this was only the start of the contractions and they were due to get much worse, the very real fear she wouldn't be able to cope made her heart pound and her head spin. Could she survive this? *Would* she?

'We've got to get you to hospital,' Max muttered, staring around, his eyes wild.

'No shit, Sherlock. Oh, fu—'

Another pain ripped through her, all-consuming, leaving her no room to think of anything else except to ride it out. As its grip tightened, she could hear herself moaning, the noise building to a crescendo, and she had an awful premonition she was about to die, torn apart from the inside out. Her knees gave way.

'No, not down there, not on the floor.' Max fought to keep her upright as she slid down the glass.

'I've got to…' she panted.

'Help! Someone help! Ian? *Ian!*'

Cynthia got onto all fours, her back hunched slightly, her head down. She could feel the baby's imperative need to be born, pushing its way out, the pressure down below so great she thought it might pop out right here, right now, on the polished tiles of the echoing foyer.

'Call an ambulance,' she cried. 'I've got to push.'

'You can't. Not here.'

'Oh, sorry, I'll tell it to stop, shall I? Arggg.' Her cry was halfway between a grunt and a scream. 'Get my tights off.'

'Pardon?'

'Get them off!

'No, I— No!'

'You're bloody useless,' she snarled, sitting back on her haunches and hiking her dress up.

'You're serious, aren't you? The baby is coming now.'

'Give the man a medal.'

'Right, let me help you. Don't move, I'm going to fetch the cushions off the sofas. You can't lie on the bare floor.' Suddenly Max had gone from panic to brisk efficiency, and by the time another contraction had swept through her, he had arranged the leather seat pads next to her. He helped her shuffle onto them.

'Lie down on your back, so I can get these off,' he commanded. Cynthia led down and lifted her bum enough for him to ease her maternity tights over her bump and down her legs. He pulled them off and tossed them to one side.

'Knickers,' she grunted.

Without a murmur, he did the same with her underwear.

She reached down as best she could and felt her nether regions. 'Can you see the head?'

Max leant forward and peered between her legs. 'I can see hair.'

She snarled. As if she had been bothered about shaving down there when she could hardly see to get her socks on. Pubic hair had been way down on the list of personal grooming lately.

He straightened up and put his phone to his ear. 'Ambulance, please.' He paused. 'Yes, the patient is breathing. And she's conscious. She's in labour, and I think the baby's head is almost out.'

Oh, *that* hair. Her baby had *hair*? Wonderf—

'I've got to push,' she told him, then bared her teeth, screwed up her eyes and pushed. There was the most extraordinary feeling as the head popped out. Her scream of triumph bounced off the walls.

'Stop! Stop pushing,' Max instructed, the phone still clamped to the side of his face.

'I can't.'

'You must, I've got to check the cord isn't wrapped around the baby's neck.'

Panting fast and hard, Cynthia stopped pushing; she could feel another contraction building though and instinctively she knew she wouldn't be able to resist its demands. 'Quick.'

He fiddled around for a second. 'No cord,' he said into the phone. 'The head is facing up, I can see the baby's eyes and nose.' In the silence between her laboured breaths, she could hear the tinny voice on the other end.

'Here it comes,' she warned, and Max hastily took his jacket off and bundled it beneath her bottom.

'The ambulance is on its way,' he informed her, 'but it's not going to get here in time. You're going to have to put up with me.'

Cynthia didn't care. She just wanted this baby out. *Now!*

With an almighty scream, she curled up, her hands gripping her knees, her chin buried in her chest, and she pushed with all her might.

The little body slithered from her, in a squelching gush.

Cynthia dropped back onto the cushions, spent. 'Is she all right?'

'Yes,' he said after far too long a pause, and there was something in his voice…

Max had wrapped the infant in his jacket, and he held the baby out to her.

She could see the little chest rise and fall, and the newborn's eyes were open. 'Give her to me,' she demanded, holding out her arms, her overwhelming weariness swept aside by intense joy and the desperate need to hold her baby. Love rose up like a tidal wave and crashed over her, and she willingly gave herself up to the incredible feeling.

'Here,' he said, 'but I warn you, she isn't a she. Unless I'm very much mistaken, you've got a son.'

Chapter 37

'A boy?'

Max nodded, carefully placing the child in her arms, his grin almost splitting his face in two. 'He's perfect.'

Cynthia gazed down at the baby in wonder. The baby gazed solemnly back. Max was right, he *was* perfect. She lifted the material away from him to check his little feet and even littler toes. And the tell-tale tiny penis nestling between his legs.

The cord was still attached, and as she examined it another weaker contraction gripped her, and a mass of yuck slipped out. Ew. Gross.

Suddenly a man's voice said loudly, 'What the hell's going on here, and who's going to clean up this mess!'

'Ian, thank God! Where have you been?' Max said. 'Can you unlock the door, please; an ambulance should be here any minute.'

Cynthia was happy for him to take charge, her full attention on the tiny baby in her arms.

She wrapped him up again, anxious he might get cold. The worry that he was four weeks too early was gnawing at her mind. Nothing else mattered except that her son (her *son*) was OK.

'Hurry, hurry,' she muttered under her breath, willing the paramedics to arrive. Even as she was whispering the words, she heard the faint sound of a siren, growing gradually louder.

'Miss Smart?' Ian was standing a few feet away, his face creased in worry. The baby gave a bleating cry and her heart constricted.

'Unlock the door, Ian. I'm sorry about the mess.'

'You've had the baby.'

She nodded; so she had.

'And in my foyer, too. Well, I never.' Scratching his head, he went to unlock the door.

Max stayed by her side, his presence calming her. Worry and elation were odd bedfellows, and she wasn't entirely sure what she was feeling – apart from the intense and overwhelming love filling her chest until she thought she might explode from it.

She couldn't take her eyes off her baby, not even when two paramedics appeared and one of them gently lifted the infant out of her arms and checked him over. The other concentrated on her.

She was hardly aware of their questions and ministrations – her focus was on her son and everything else faded into insignificance as the paramedics prepared to transfer the pair of them to the hospital.

'Is he all right?' she asked, her voice catching. She felt Max's hand on her shoulder and was grateful for his presence. She was grateful to him for a lot of things tonight.

'He's fine,' the paramedic assured her. 'Let's get you both to hospital where you can be checked over properly.'

Cynthia sent Max a panicked look.

'I'll follow in my car,' he promised, and she had to be satisfied with that, despite the fact that she really wanted him to stay with her.

He was true to his word, and she hadn't been in the hospital long before he stuck his head around the door. They'd put her in one of the labour suites, and she was feeling rather overwhelmed at the amount of to-ing and fro-ing, prodding and poking, and all the questions, so she was relieved to see him.

She laughed out loud, a gulping sobbing noise, when he sidled into the room, a silly grin on his face and a balloon hidden behind his back.

Not very well hidden, because she could see the top of it bobbing above his head.

'Congratulations,' he said. 'Where is the little guy?'

Cynthia's eyes filled, and she dashed the trickle of tears from her cheeks. 'They've taken him to the neonatal unit for observation,' she told him.

'But he's OK, isn't he?'

'So they tell me. I just want to be with him.' She was having real difficulty trying to steady herself. In the space of a minute, she alternated between wanting to laugh, to cry, and to scream.

'Come here.' Max gathered her up, holding her close. She could smell his aftershave and the cold fresh air of the outside on his shirt.

'Your jacket,' she remembered, then the tears overwhelmed the laughter and she cried in earnest.

He continued to hold her, stroking her hair, and she drew from his quiet strength, using it to prop up her own depleted reserves.

'Thank you,' she said eventually, pulling away to wipe her face and blow her nose.

'I'm just glad I arrived when I did.'

'Why were you there?'

'I told you – I came to see you.'

'I gathered that, but you didn't say why.' She turned her attention to one of the midwives (she had yet to see Jess, although it was rather late now, considering her services were no longer needed). 'Can I see my baby?'

'We'll admit you to a ward for tonight, and as soon as we've sorted out a bed for you we'll get someone to take you to the neonatal unit.'

Cynthia drooped. How long was that going to take? She was desperate to hold him – her arms felt so empty. A direct contrast to her heart, which was so full she thought it might burst, and her boobs which were leaking fluid and making her bra feel sticky and uncomfortable, a small ache to add to her list of woes.

She hadn't even fed her baby yet, and the knowledge made her wail anew.

Max was there once more, wrapping her in his strong embrace and murmuring that everything would be all right.

She so desperately wanted to believe him.

'Right, my sweetie,' one of the midwives said. 'We've got a bed for you. On the way to the ward, I'll arrange for you to be taken via the neonatal unit, and you can spend a few minutes with your baby. The staff will probably want to get some colostrum into him, so they'll see if you can feed him, or maybe express. But don't worry,' she added hastily, as Cynthia began to panic, 'they'll help you to do that. Dad, would you like to go with her? I'm sure you must be desperate to see your little boy.'

Max bent his head to look at Cynthia.

'If you want,' she said. 'Please don't feel obliged.'

'Oh, but I am. I've got a vested interest. I want to check on my handiwork.'

She gave him the ghost of a smile. 'I don't know what I'd have done without you.'

'You'd have coped. You're a strong, independent woman.'

'I don't feel strong right now,' she replied. She wasn't sure about the independent bit, either. 'Why did you want to see me?' she asked again.

'It doesn't matter. I'll tell you later, when things have calmed down a bit. Ah, here's your ride.'

Max stepped aside to let the porter wheel her out of the labour suite, a nurse accompanying them, and he followed behind. She could sense him there, his rock-steady presence making her feel warm and safe. If it wasn't for him, she might still be in Sally's office, on her own with a brand new baby. Or worse. The cord hadn't been around the baby's neck, but what if it had been and she'd been alone?

Max had been an absolute hero and she knew she couldn't thank him enough. The least she could do, she thought randomly, was to buy him a new jacket.

Her baby was wrapped in a blanket and lying in an incubator. He was also yelling at the top of his voice and was evidently furious about something.

'Why is he crying? What's wrong with him?' Cynthia asked frantically.

'He's hungry and he wants his mum.' A nurse stepped forward. 'He's a strong wee lad, a bit early, but not too much. How do you feel about feeding him?'

Cynthia couldn't think of anything else she'd prefer to do.

The nurse helped her sit forward and pull her dress up – she must ask someone (Sally?) to pop into her flat and fetch her some clean, and more suitable, clothes. A toothbrush would be good, too. Then she watched avidly as her baby was gently removed from the incubator and placed in her arms. He quietened immediately and began rooting.

'He can smell the milk,' the nurse said.

He felt solid and delicate at the same time. To think only an hour or so ago, he'd been safely curled in her womb, and now here he was – her very own baby.

She gazed at the mop of black hair, the crunched up, slightly squashed face, the button nose, those far-too aware and knowing eyes, and her heart constricted. He was gorgeous, perfect and wonderful, and she knew she would lay down her life for him without question.

With a little bit of help from the nurse, the baby latched on, Cynthia's toes curling at the surprisingly strong suck. Ooh, that felt weird – it felt right too, and she took deep joy from knowing she was providing sustenance to her baby.

His little lips worked at her nipple and his eyes were closed, and she revelled in the smell of him, and the soft snuffling sounds he was making, and the very sight of him calmed her. She could do this. She *was* doing this.

Finally, she felt him relax, the sucking trailed off and the nipple slipped out of his mouth.

With a huge smile, she looked up, triumphant, proud, and blissfully happy.

Her eyes met Max's. His expression was also proud, and soft too, tenderness radiating from him like a warmth she could almost reach out and touch.

And a thought struck her – a thought so powerful she nearly cried out; this man should have been her baby's father. She loved him, and if she hadn't known any better she could have sworn by the look in his eyes that he loved her, too.

Chapter 38

Cynthia sat in the passenger seat of Max's car and sobbed into a tissue. As she sobbed, she was aware she was being ridiculous. She'd fed her baby this morning, she'd visit him again this afternoon. If he was still making good progress, he might be allowed home tomorrow.

So why was she bawling her eyes out?

She could have stayed by his side all day (she certainly *wanted* to), but she needed to return to her apartment to ensure everything was ready for his arrival. For God's sake, she didn't even have any nappies!

She trusted Max to fetch what was needed, but he'd already done so much and she didn't feel she could impose on him anymore.

There was, however, one thing she was going to ask him to do, and that was to put the bloody cot together, because it was still in bits on the nursery floor.

First, though, he insisted they stopped off at a supermarket so he could make sure she had enough supplies in for a few days, at least. He'd nipped off to her apartment last night and had brought her back some night things, toiletries, and some clean clothes for this morning, without being asked. His thoughtfulness had reduced her to tears (*again*), but all he'd been concerned about was that she didn't have a great deal in her fridge.

To be fair, she'd not expected to need a "great deal". She always grabbed breakfast on the way to work, her lunch was a sandwich from the deli across the street, and the range of take away food from her local Just Eateries was impressive, and not all of it fast food, which did her for dinner. She had been planning on ordering a mushroom risotto with a side salad last night. As that was how she usually fed herself and the baby hadn't been supposed to arrive for four more weeks, she didn't see the point in stocking her fridge and cupboards with food she neither had the time nor the inclination to cook.

She sat in the car while he freed a trolley from its mates and prepared to do battle inside, and she thought how lucky she was he was here. Not only had he driven to the hospital behind the ambulance; he'd stuck around. He was still sticking around, and she hoped it was because he was one of the good guys.

Oh, hell, she hadn't phoned her mum.

By the time she was settled last night, safely tucked up in her own room in a side ward, her breasts uncomfortable and her nether regions sore, listening to the cries of tiny babies and the soothing tones of their mothers and the hospital staff, it was too late to call. Her mother wasn't getting any younger, and a phone call in the middle of the night wouldn't be good for her, no matter how fantastic the news.

Jess had popped in to see her this morning as she was eating breakfast, and Cynthia had explained how her birth plan hadn't gone according to plan, and she'd had a bit of a midwife crisis until Max had stepped in and had delivered her baby.

'He's better looking than me,' Jess had joked, 'and I heard he did as good a job.'

'I don't mind *you* peering at my bits and pieces,' Cynthia had said, 'but not Max. It's probably put him off sex for life, and even if it hasn't, he's bound to be traumatised. I could have done without him delving around down there. Helping me deliver my baby wasn't the way I envisioned us getting up close and personal for the first time.'

'Ooh, so you *have* thought about doing the dirty with hunky Max. I thought you said he was just a colleague?'

Cynthia had felt her cheeks grow warm and she'd hastily changed the subject.

By the time she was up and dressed, had fed the baby, and was back in her room, the doctor had completed his rounds and she was being discharged. Max, bless him, had turned up just as she was contemplating getting a taxi.

So, there she was, sitting in his car, sniffing and snivelling, and hoping he would buy skimmed milk and not semi because she needed to lose her horrid flabby tummy as soon as possible.

Filled with quiet excitement, she rang her mum.

'My baby isn't a girl,' she announced without preamble. 'It's a boy.'

'I knew it!' her mum cried. 'Don't go buying anything blue, though, because these scan thingies have been known to get it wrong.'

'It's definitely a boy. He arrived last night. Six pounds, two ounces in old money.' Cynthia laughed as her mum gave an almighty squeal, and she held the phone away from her ear. When she put it back again, it was to hear her mother demanding to know if the baby was all right.

'He's adorable, Mum, and absolutely perfect.'

'Of course he is! Ooh, I can't wait to see him. And how are you?' Cynthia heard the worry behind the question.

'Shocked, sore,' she began, then recounted the events of the previous night.

'Max! Your Max?' her mum cried, when Cynthia had finished telling her. 'Well, I never!'

'He's not my Max.'

'He should be, after that. I told you he has feelings for you.'

'He might have, but I didn't feel I could trust him.'

'And now?'

'We'll have to see. Can I still come to yours?' She smiled up at Max as he opened the door, a full trolley next to him. She hadn't been entirely truthful with her mum – she should have told her she trusted Max with her life. After all, she'd trusted him with that of her baby's.

'Everything OK?' he mouthed and she nodded.

'Of course you can,' her mum said. 'When do you think you'll be allowed to bring him home?'

'I'm hoping it'll be tomorrow, but we'll have to see. I'll need to sort my car out, too, before I drive down to yours.' She swivelled around to watch Max load up the boot. At the moment, she could hardly sit down, let alone drive.

'You *still* haven't swapped it for something else?' Maggie demanded

'No, I thought I had a couple of weeks to go yet.'

263

'Oh, my darling, didn't anyone tell you babies have their own agendas?'

Evidently not. Or if they had, she hadn't been listening. 'I'll be with you as soon as I can, but I don't want to try to stuff the baby and all the gear into a tiny sports car.'

'I can drive you,' Max offered.

'I'll need my own transport when I'm in Little Milling,' she said. 'Thank you, anyway.'

'How about if you drive my car and I'll drive yours. Then when you feel up to it, your mum can look after the baby for a couple of hours, while you see about getting a part-exchange.'

'You'd do that for me?'

He shrugged, and a faint hint of pink spread across his high cheekbones.

'Why?' she persisted.

'Because.'

'That's not an answer.'

'It'll have to do.'

'What did you want to talk to me about last night?' She narrowed her eyes. 'Did Sally have anything to do with you turning up?'

'She might have.'

He focused on starting the engine and looking in the mirrors.

'You'd better tell me; I'll find out anyway,' she warned.

'After your scare in the hospital, I came looking for you. You wouldn't answer my calls or my texts.'

Cynthia winced. She must remember to unblock him.

'Sally said you were off sick,' he continued, 'so I tried your apartment, and when I didn't get any joy, I called into your mum's on the way back to Greenleaves. You weren't there, either; or so she said.' He glanced at her. 'I was going to try to forget all about you. You evidently didn't want anything to do with me, and I tried to respect that.'

'What changed your mind?'

'Sally. She sent me an email. It was sheer luck I got it because for some reason it went into my spam folder. See, even my email provider doesn't like the Wallace Corporation,' he said.

'What did it say?' She was listening to him with wide eyes and bated breath.

'Before I tell you, please be aware she only did what she thought was best, OK? So don't give her any grief,' he warned.

'I'm not going to. If you hadn't been there last night…'

'Yeah, well.' He coloured even more. 'She said you were back in London, and she thought you still had feelings for me. She said you were hurting and had some trust issues, but I shouldn't give up.'

'And you didn't.'

'I phoned her the second I read it. Because I hadn't replied, she'd assumed I didn't want to know, but once I explained about the spam folder, she told me everything,' he said with a soft smile. 'I was hoping to catch you before you left work for the day, because I thought if I approached you in the office you wouldn't want to make a scene and slam the door in my face, and I'd have a better chance of making you listen to me.'

'Don't count on it,' she said, but she was smiling. She reached across the small space between them and stroked his arm. He sent her a slow smile.

'The traffic was awful and by the time I arrived, everyone had gone,' he said. 'I called Sally and told her I'd missed you, and that I'd try to catch you at home. Then I had a text from her to say you were still in the office, and that she'd do her best to keep you there for a couple of minutes.'

'The little madam. She didn't lose her necklace at all.'

'Pardon?'

'I was rooting around under her desk searching for the necklace she said she'd lost, when you appeared.'

'I wondered what you were doing on the floor.'

'About to have a baby, apparently,' she teased. God, but she was missing her son, and she couldn't wait to get back to the hospital. She could smell his delicious baby scent on her clothes, and if she concentrated she could still feel the weight of him in her arms.

'What were you going to say to me when you saw me?' she asked.

'That the job is still there if you want it. That I meant what I said when I told you I have no interest in Ricky's company. That I'm sorry if you think I misled you, but Ricky wanted to keep it quiet until things were confirmed. I agreed, because I didn't want people treating me like the boss's son, especially since I was pretty certain I didn't want to run the company. He might be a shit, but he's my father. I felt I owed it to him to give it a fair crack of the whip.'

'How did he take it when you told him?'

Max shrugged. 'Surprisingly well. Disappointed obviously. How did you take it?'

'What do you mean?'

He indicated to turn right and waited for the traffic to let him through. 'The way is clear for you, if you want it. He doesn't have anyone else.'

'I don't want it. I want a job where I can leave before eight p.m. and not be slated for it. I was planning on looking for something else, something more compatible with raising a child.'

'I've got just the job for you,' he said, softly.

'Can I think about it?'

'As I've said before, take as long as you need. I'm just glad we're on speaking terms again.'

She didn't have to think about it (she'd done so much thinking over the past few months her head was spinning) but she did need to make doubly certain this was the right thing to do, both for her and her baby.

'There's something else,' he said, pulling into a rare parking space outside her apartment. 'I'm not trying to influence your decision, but you can have my cottage.'

Cynthia inhaled sharply, not sure if she'd heard him correctly.

He switched off the engine and held up his hands. 'OK, maybe I am trying to sweeten the deal, but I know you are worried about accommodation, and living with your mum long term isn't ideal.'

'What's the rent?'

He hesitated. 'Let's just say, you'll be more than able to afford it on the salary I'll be paying you. And it also means you don't have to sell your apartment. I think it's probably a good idea if you don't. Renting it out should cover your mortgage, and it'll be a good investment for the future.'

'I don't have a mortgage on it.'

He smiled. 'Even better, it'll be extra income for you.'

It sounded like a plan, but Cynthia knew from recent experience that plans often went the way of Robbie Burns – "aft agley". She needed to look into it fully.

Oh, who was she kidding! What she seriously needed to consider was whether she could live and work in the same place as Max, seeing him every day, loving him every day, and not having him love her in return.

Could she do it?

'There's something else,' he said.

'How many more somethings are you going to throw my way?'

'As many as it takes, to persuade you.'

'What is it?'

'I love you.'

Cynthia's mouth dropped open. She shook her head in disbelief. 'I've just given birth.'

'I know, I was there.'

'You've seen me…' She pulled a face.

'So?'

'Evan is another man's child.'

'Evan? Is that his name? I like it. And I repeat – so?'

'Do you really love me?'

'I do.'

'When?'

'When what?' He took her hand in his.

'When did you know?'

'The first time I laid eyes on you.'

Her heart swelled with joy. It seemed like she had two new men in her life. 'I might have feelings for you, too,' she admitted, shyly.

'Good. I'd hate for my love to be unrequited. Does that mean you'll say yes?'

'It doesn't. I still need to think about it.'

'I'll wait.' He squeezed her hand, his face breaking into a smile.

'I've got a few conditions,' she said.

The smile faded a little. 'OK.'

'I want a contract, a proper one, both for the job and the cottage.'

'You've got it. Next?'

'How good are you at putting cots together?'

'Never tried,' he replied cheerfully. 'But how hard can it be?'

Oh, matey, she thought, you've got a lot to learn. Then she leant towards him, the gear stick sticking into her wobbly tummy, and she kissed him.

It was a long time before either of them thought about putting a cot together.

Chapter 39

'Evan! Take that out of your mouth.' Cynthia sent her mum an apologetic look. 'He's at the stage where he bites anything he can get his hands on.' In this instance it was Maggie's reading glasses, which she'd left within reach of pudgy fingers.

'If you think you've got your work cut out for you now, wait until he starts walking,' her mum warned. 'It'll keep you fit. Not that you need it,' she added.

Cynthia smoothed a hand down over her tummy. It wasn't as flat as it had been before she had Evan and she suspected it never would be, but it would do. From the way Max trailed kisses over it on a regular basis, the shape of it didn't seem to worry him at all.

As if her mum could read her mind, Maggie said, 'I expected to see Max.' She looked around the cosy living room, hopefully.

'He's not hiding behind the sofa, Mum. He's at the hotel.'

'Still?'

'I don't follow. He works there, he owns the business. Why wouldn't he be there?'

'It doesn't mean to say he has to live there too, not when there's a perfectly good cottage here.'

'*I* live here with Evan, or have you forgotten?'

Maggie gave her a sideways look. 'I bet he stays here more often than not. Why don't you put the poor man out of his misery and ask him to move back into his own house?'

'Why don't you mind your own business?' Cynthia muttered under her breath as she wiped the dribble from her son's face. His cheeks were far rosier than the temperature in the living room warranted and she guessed he was teething again. Another restless night for her was looming.

'He's besotted by you,' her mother was saying. 'And if I'm not mistaken, you're head over heels in love with him too. What are you waiting for? You're not getting any younger, you know.'

'Thanks for the reminder. I'm not old yet.'

'You soon will be. It's scary how fast time flies, and it gets quicker the older you get. Before you know it, little Evan here will be off to university and that man of yours will have got fed up of waiting for you and will be installing someone else in his cottage.'

Evan at eighteen? It didn't bear thinking about. That would make her sixty-three!

'Max isn't going to install anyone else in the cottage. Anyway, he'll be sixty-four by then.'

'Just because one has retired doesn't mean one is past-it, romantically speaking,' her mother retorted, loftily.

Cynthia cocked her head, and scrutinised her mother. There was a sparkle in her eye and a rosy glow on her cheeks. 'You sly old thing,' she said slowly. 'Who is he?'

'Mr Williams, next door.'

'The one you take meals to?'

'Yes.' Maggie lifted her chin.

'Good for you!

'Now, then, if I can do it, so can you.'

'I am already "doing it", Mum.'

'Don't be vulgar. I meant move in with him. Mr Williams is going to move in with me.'

Good Lord! Did her mum still call him Mr Williams when they were in bed together? Ew, that was a thought too far, and Cynthia shoved it away with a grimace.

'Young lady,' her mum said. 'You love him, he loves you. He also adores that son of yours, and that's not to be sneezed at.'

'I'm not sneezing. I am thankful and grateful he treats Evan as though he were his own child.'

'Then why don't you let him be a proper father to him, and live with you?'

'Because I don't want him for his parenting qualities. I want him for him. Besides, he hasn't asked me.'

'Asked you what?'

'To marry me.'

'Is that what's holding you back? Not having a ring on your finger?'

Cynthia pulled a pout.

'Then why don't I go ahead and put one on there?' a masculine voice said from behind, and she squeaked and leapt to her feet.

Max was lounging against the doorjamb, with a can of beer in his hand and a smirk on his handsome face.

'How long have you been standing there?' she demanded.

'Long enough.'

Dear God... he'd heard it all.

Suddenly he was on one knee and holding out a ring-pull. 'This wasn't how I envisioned this, but I'm here now and I truly would like to spend the rest of my life with you, and not flitting back and fore between the hotel and the cottage.' He took a deep breath. 'Cynthia Smart, will you marry me?'

'Yes! Yes!' She shoved her finger at him, and he slipped the ring pull onto it. She noticed his hand was shaking ever so slightly and she loved him all the more for his uncertainty.

'Did I ever thank you for playing midwife?' she murmured into his neck as he scooped her up and cuddled her to him, and she thanked her lucky stars he'd come to find her that night and she'd seen first-hand what a wonderfully caring man he was.

'Nope. Not once.'

'Then I'd better thank you properly later,' she whispered, keeping her voice as low as she could so her mother couldn't hear.

'I'll look forward to it. And I'm looking forward to the rest of our lives together,' he added, his mouth in her hair.

Her mum piped up, 'I *can* hear you. Now, about that silly sports car you still haven't got rid of. How about if I buy it off you? I feel like having a midlife crisis of my own. Whoever said life begins at forty needs to look seventy in the face. Right then, when's the wedding? I need to buy a hat.'

Cynthia collapsed into giggles, happiness filling every part of her. Not only did she have a scatty mother who had found her second wind, a cute, cheerful, chubby son, a gorgeous cottage to live in, a job she loved, and a best friend in Lara, but she had a wonderful man who she adored and who wanted to marry her.

Life, for Cynthia Smart, couldn't get any better.

THE END

About the Author

Liz Davies writes feel-good, light-hearted stories with a hefty dose of romance, a smattering of humour, and a great deal of love.

She's married to her best friend, has a grown-up daughter, and when she isn't scribbling away in the notepad she carries with her everywhere (just in case inspiration strikes), you'll find her searching for that perfect pair of shoes. She loves to cook but isn't very good at it, and loves to eat - she's much better at that! Liz also enjoys walking (preferably on the flat), cycling (also on the flat), and lots of sitting around in the garden on warm, sunny days.

She currently lives with her family in Wales, but would ideally love to buy a camper van and travel the world in it.

If you'd like to see what else she's written, then head on over to her website elizabethdaviesauthor.co.uk

Or you can find her on
Twitter: lizdaviesauthor
Facebook: LizDaviesAuthor1

Printed in Poland
by Amazon Fulfillment
Poland Sp. z o.o., Wrocław
06 September 2023

3b93e993-31d3-417c-91e2-0d945309e7b4R01